The Wizard of Oz Collection

Book Fifteen

The Royal Book of Oz

Ruth Plumly Thompson

Founded on the Oz series by L. Frank Baum

Contents

Published by Sweet Cherry Publishing Limited
Unit E, Vulcan Business Complex
Vulcan Road,
Leicester, LE5 3EB
United Kingdom

www.sweetcherrypublishing.com

Title: The Royal Book of Oz
UK Edition

The Royal Book of Oz originally published in 1921
This edition first published in the UK in 2014
ISBN: 978-1-78226-107-0

Cover designed by Kingshuk Chaudhary,
© Creative Books

Printed in India by Ajanta Offset and Packagings Limited

Author's Note

Dear Children,

You will remember that, in the front part of Glinda of Oz, the Publishers told you that when Mr Baum went away from this world he left behind some unfinished notes about the Princess Ozma and Dorothy and the jolly people of the Wonderful Land of Oz. The Publishers promised that they would try to put these notes together into a new Oz book for you.

Well, here it is – The Royal Book of Oz.

I am sure that Mr Baum would be pleased that Ruth Plumly Thompson, who has known and loved the Oz stories ever since she was a little girl, has made this new Oz story, with all the Oz folks in it and true to life.

You see I am Mrs Baum, the wife of the Royal Historian of Oz, and so I know how he feels about everything.

Now, about the story:

Of course, we all knew the Scarecrow was a very fine fellow, but surely we never guessed he ascended from an emperor. Most of us descend from our ancestors, but the Scarecrow really ascended.

The Scarecrow had a most exciting and adventurous time on the Silver Isle, and Dorothy and the Cowardly Lion just ran out of one adventure into another trying to rescue him. They made some charming new friends in their travels – Sir Hokus of Pokes, the Doubtful Dromedary, and the Comfortable Camel. You'll find them very unusual and likeable. They have the same peculiar, delightful and informal natures that we love in all the queer Oz people.

This note is intended for all the children of America, who knew and loved Mr Baum, and it goes to each of you with his love and mine.

Maud G. Baum
Ozcot
Hollywood, California
In the spring, 1921.

Chapter 1

Professor Wogglebug's Great Idea

"The very thing!" exclaimed Professor Wogglebug, bounding into the air and upsetting his gold inkwell. "The very next idea!"

"Who, me?" A round-faced little Munchkin boy stuck his head in the door and regarded Professor Wogglebug solemnly. He was working his way through the Professor's Athletic college, and one of his duties was to wait upon this eminent educator of Oz.

"Certainly not!" snapped Professor Wogglebug. "You're a nobody or a nothing. Stop gaping and fetch me my hat. I'm off to the Emerald City. And mind the pupils take their history pills regularly while I'm gone," he added, clapping his tall hat Zif held out to him on the back of his head.

"Yes, sir!" said the little Munchkin respectfully.

"Don't hurry back, sir!" This last remark the Professor did not hear, for he was already half way down the college steps.

"Ozma will be delighted with the idea. How clever I am!" he murmured, twirling his antennae and walking rapidly down the pleasant blue lane.

The Professor, whose College of Art and Athletic Perfection is in the south western part of the Munchkin country, is the biggest bug in Oz, or in anyplace else, for that matter. He has made education painless by substituting school pills for books. His students take Latin, history and spelling pills; they swallow knowledge of every kind with ease and pleasure and spend the rest of their time in sport. No wonder he is so well thought of in Oz! No wonder he thinks so well of himself! Swinging his cane jauntily, the Professor hurried toward the yellow brick road that leads to the Emerald City, and by nightfall had reached the lovely capital of Oz.

Oz! That marvellous country where no one grows old, where animals and birds talk as sensibly as people, and adventures happen every day. Indeed, of all fairylands in the world, Oz is the most delightful, and of all fairy cities, the Emerald City is the most beautiful. A soft green light shone for miles about, and the gemmed turrets and spires of the palace flashed more brightly than the stars. But its loveliness was familiar to Professor Wogglebug, and without a pause he proceeded to Ozma's palace and was at once admitted to the great hall.

A roar of merriment greeted his ears. Ozma, the lovely girl ruler of Oz, was having a party, and the room was full of most surprising people, surprising to some, that is, but old friends to most of us.

Jack, holding tightly to his pumpkin head, was running as fast as his wooden feet and wobbly legs would take him from Dorothy. A game of blind-man's buff was in full swing, and Scraps and Tik-Tok, the Scarecrow and Nick Chopper, the Glass Cat and the Cowardly Lion, the Wizard of Oz and the Wooden Sawhorse, Cap'n Bill and Betsy Bobbin, Billina and the Hungry Tiger were tumbling over each other in an effort to keep away from the blindfolded little girl. But Dorothy was too quick for them. With a sudden whirl, she spun 'round and grasped a coat sleeve.

"The Scarecrow!" she laughed triumphantly. "I can tell by the way he skwoshes and now *he's* it!"

"I'm always *it!*" chuckled the droll person.

"But hah! Behold the learned Professor standing so aloofly in our midst."

No one had noticed Professor Wogglebug, who had been quietly watching the game. "I don't like to interrupt the party," he began, approaching Ozma's throne apologetically, "but I've just had a most brilliant idea!"

"What? Another?" murmured the Scarecrow, rolling up his eyes.

"Where did you lose it?" asked Jack Pumpkinhead, edging forward anxiously.

"Lose it! Who said I'd lost it?" snapped the Professor, glaring at poor
Jack.

"Well, you said you'd had it, and had is the past tense, so…" Jack's voice trailed off uncertainly, and Ozma, seeing he was embarrassed, begged the Professor to explain.

"Your Highness!" began Professor Wogglebug, while the company settled down in a resigned circle on the floor, "As Oz is the most interesting and delightful country on the Continent of Imagination and its people the most unusual and talented, I am about to compile a Royal Book which will give the names and history of all our people. In other words, I am to be the Great, Grand Genealogist of Oz!"

"Whatever that is," the Scarecrow whispered in Dorothy's ear.

"And," the Professor frowned severely on the Scarecrow, "with your
Majesty's permission, I shall start at once!"

"Please do," said the Scarecrow with a wave toward the door, "and we will go on with the party!"

Scraps, the Patchwork Girl, who had been staring fixedly at the Professor with her silver suspender-button eyes, now sprang to her feet:

"What is a genealogist?
It's something no one here has missed;
What puts such notions in your head?
Turn out your toes or go to bed!"

she shouted gaily, then, catching Ozma's disapproving glance, fell over backwards.

"I don't understand it at all," said Jack Pumpkinhead in a depressed voice. "I'm afraid my head's too ripe."

"Nor I," said Tik-Tok, the copper clockwork man. "Please wind me up a lit-tle tight-er Dor-o-thy,

I want to think!"

Dorothy obligingly took a key suspended from a hook on his back and wound him up under his left arm. Everybody began to talk at once, and what with the Cowardly Lion's deep growl and Tik-Tok's squeaky voice and all the rest of the tin and meat and wooden voices, the confusion was terrible.

"Wait!" cried Ozma, clapping her hands. Immediately the room grew so still that one could hear Tik-Tok's machinery whirring 'round. "Now!" said Ozma, "One at a time, please, and let us hear from the Scarecrow first."

The Scarecrow rose. "I think, your Highness," he said modestly, "that anyone who has studied his Geozify already knows who we are and-"

"Who you are?" broke in the Wogglebug scornfully, "Of course they do. But *I* shall tell them who you *were*!"

"Who I were?" gasped the Scarecrow in a dazed voice, raising his cotton glove to his forehead. "Who I were? Well, who were I?"

"That's just the point," said Professor Wogglebug. "Who were you? Who were your ancestors? Where is your family? Where is your family tree? From what did you descend?"

At each question, the Scarecrow looked more embarrassed. He repeated the last one several times. "From what did I descend? From what did I descend? Why, from a bean pole!" he cried.

This was perfectly true, for Dorothy, a little girl blown by a Kansas cyclone to the Kingdom of Oz, had discovered the Scarecrow in a farmer's cornfield and had lifted him down from his pole. Together they had made the journey to the Emerald City, where the Wizard of Oz had fitted him out with a fine set of brains. At one time, he had ruled Oz and was generally considered its cleverest citizen.

Before he could reply further, the Patchwork Girl, who was simply irrepressible, burst out:

"An ex-straw-ordinary man is he!
A bean pole for his family tree,
A Cornishman, upon my soul,
Descended from a tall, thin Pole!"

"Nonsense!" said Professor Wogglebug sharply, "Being stuffed with straw may make him extraordinary, but it is quite plain that the Scarecrow was nobody before he was himself. He has no ancestors, no family; only a bean pole for a family tree, and is therefore entitled to the merest mention in the Royal Book of Oz!"

"How about my brains?" asked the Scarecrow in a hurt voice. "Aren't they enough?"

"Brains have simply nothing to do with royalty!" Professor Wogglebug waved his fountain pen firmly. "Now-"

"But see here, wasn't I Ruler of Oz?" put in the Scarecrow anxiously.

"A Ruler but *never* a royalty!" snapped out the Professor. "Now, if you will all answer my questions as I call your names, I'll get the necessary data and be off." He took out a small memorandum book. "Your Highness," he bowed to Ozma, "need not bother. I have already entered your name at the head of the list. Being descended as you are from a long line of fairies, your family tree is the oldest and most illustrious in Oz, Princess Dorothy!"

At the sound of her name, the little girl stood up.

"I know you are from Kansas and were created a Princess of Oz by our gracious Ruler, but can you tell me anything of your ancestors in America?" demanded the Professor, staring over the top of his thick glasses.

"You'll have to ask Uncle Henry and Aunt Em," said Dorothy rather sulkily.

The Professor had hurt the feelings of her best friend, the Scarecrow, and ancestors did not interest her one little bit.

"Very well," said the Professor, writing industriously in his book. "I'll just enter you as 'Dorothy, Princess of Oz and sixth cousin to a President!'"

"I'm not!" Dorothy shook her head positively.

"Oh, everyone in America can claim that!" said the Professor easily.

"Nick Chopper!"

Now up rose our old friend the Tin Woodman, who had also been discovered by Dorothy on her first trip to the Fairyland of Oz.

"You were a man of meat at one time and a woodman by trade?" queried Professor Wogglebug, poising his pen in the air.

"I am a Tin Woodman, and you may enter me in your book under the name of Smith, for a tin Smith made me, and as Royal Emperor of the Winkies, I do not care to go back to my meat connections," said the Tin Woodman in a dignified voice.

The company applauded, and the Cowardly

Lion thumped the floor with his tail.

"Smith is a very good name. I can work up a whole chapter on that," smiled the Professor. The Tin Woodman *had* once been a regular person, but a wicked witch enchanted his axe, and first it chopped off one leg, then the other, and next both arms and his head. After each accident, Nick went to a tinsmith for repairs, and finally was entirely made of tin. Nowhere but in Oz could such a thing happen. But no one can be killed in this marvellous country, and Nick, with his tin body, went gaily on living and was considered so distinguished that the Winkies had begged him to be their Emperor.

"Scraps!" called the Professor as Nick sat stiffly down beside Dorothy.

The Patchwork Girl pirouetted madly to the front. Putting one finger in her mouth, she sang:

> *"I'm made of patches, as you see.*
> *A clothes tree is my family tree*
> *But, pshaw! It's all the same to me!"*

A clothes tree? Even Professor Wogglebug grinned. Who could help laughing at Scraps? Made of odd pieces of goods and brought to life by the powder of life, the comical girl was the jolliest person imaginable.

"Put me down as a man of me-tal!" drawled Tik-Tok the copper man as the laugh following Scraps' rhyme had subsided. Tik-Tok was still another of Dorothy's discoveries, and this marvellous machine man, guaranteed to last a thousand years, could think, walk, and talk when properly wound.

The Cowardly Lion was entered as a King in his own right. One after the other, the celebrities of Oz came forward to answer Professor Wogglebug's questions. The Professor wrote rapidly in his little book. Ozma listened attentively to each one, and they all seemed interested except the Scarecrow. Slumped down beside Dorothy, he stared morosely at the ceiling, his jolly face all wrinkled down on one side.

"If I only knew who I were!" he muttered over and over. "I must think!"

"Don't you mind." Dorothy patted his shoulder kindly. "Royalties are out of date, and I'll bet the Professor's family tree was a milkweed!"

But the Scarecrow refused to be comforted, and long after the company had retired he sat hunched sadly in his corner. "I'll do it! I'll do it!"

he exclaimed at last, rising unsteadily to his feet. Jellia Jamb, Ozma's little waiting maid, returning somewhat later to fetch a handkerchief her mistress had dropped, was surprised to see him running through the long hall.

"Why, where are you going?" asked Jellia.

"To find my family tree!" said the Scarecrow darkly, and drawing himself up to his full height, he fell through the doorway.

Chapter 2

The Scarecrow's Family Tree

The moon shone brightly, but everyone in the Emerald City was fast asleep! Through the deserted streets hurried the Scarecrow. For the first time since his discovery by little Dorothy, he was really unhappy. Living as he did in a Fairyland, he had taken many things for granted and had rather prided himself on his unusual appearance. Indeed, not until Professor Wogglebug's rude remarks concerning his family had he given his past a thought.

"I am the only person in Oz without a family!" he reflected sorrowfully. "Even the Cowardly Lion has kingly parents and a palm tree! But I must keep thinking. My brains have never failed me yet. Who was I? Who were I? Who were I?"

Often he thought so hard that he forgot to look where he was going and ran headlong into fences, stumbled down gutters, and over stiles. But fortunately, the dear fellow could not hurt himself, and he would struggle up, pat his straw into shape, and walk straightway into something else. He made good time in between falls, however, and was soon well on his way down the yellow brick road that ran through the Munchkin Country. For he had determined to return to the Munchkin farm where Dorothy had first discovered him and try to find some traces of his family.

Now being stuffed with straw had many advantages, for requiring neither food nor sleep the Scarecrow could travel night and day without interruption. The stars winked out one by one, and by the time the cocks of the Munchkin farmers began to crow, he had come to the banks of a broad blue river!

The Scarecrow took off his hat and scratched his head thoughtfully. Crossing rivers is no easy matter in Oz, for there isn't a ferry in the Kingdom, and unless one is a good swimmer or equipped with some of the Wizard's magic it is mighty troublesome. Water does not agree with the Scarecrow at all, and as for swimming, he can no more swim than a bag of meal.

But he was too wise a person to give up merely because a thing appeared to be impossible. It was for just such emergencies that his excellent brains had been given to him.

"If Nick Chopper were here, he would build a raft in no time," murmured the Scarecrow, "but as he is not, I must think of another way!"

Turning his back on the river, which distracted his mind, he began to think with all his might. Before he could collect his thoughts, there was a tremendous crash, and next minute he was lying face down in the mud. Several little crashes followed, and a shower of water. Then a wet voice called out with a cheerful chuckle:

"Come on out, my dear Rattles. Not a bad place at all, and here's breakfast already waiting!"

"Breakfast!" The Scarecrow turned over cautiously. A huge and curious creature was slashing through the grass toward him. A smaller and still more curious one followed. Both were extremely damp and had evidently just come out of the river.

"Good morning!" quavered the Scarecrow, sitting up with a jerk and at the same time reaching for a stick that lay just behind him.

"I won't eat it if it talks - so there!" The smaller

creature stopped and stared fixedly at the Scarecrow.

The Scarecrow, hearing this, tried to think of something else to say, but the appearance of the two was so amazing that, as he told Dorothy afterwards, he was struck dumb. The larger was at least two hundred feet long and made entirely of blocks of wood. On each block was a letter of the alphabet. The head was a huge square block with a serpent's face and long, curling, tape-measure tongue. The little one was very much smaller and seemed to consist of hundreds of rattles, wood, celluloid, and rubber, fastened together with wires. Every time it moved, the rattles tinkled. Its face, however, was not unpleasant, so the Scarecrow took heart and made a deep bow.

"And I'm not going to eat anything that squirms." This time it was the big serpent who spoke.

"Thank you!" said the Scarecrow, bowing several times more. "You relieve my mind. I've never been a breakfast yet, and I'd rather not begin. But if I cannot be your breakfast, let me be your friend!" He extended his arms impulsively.

There was something so jolly about the Scarecrow's smile that the two creatures became friendly at once, and moreover told him the story of their lives.

"As you have doubtless noted," began the larger creature, "I am an A-B-Sea Serpent. I am employed in the nursery of the Mer children to teach them their letters. My friend, here, is a Rattlesnake, and it is his business to amuse the Mer babies while the Mermaids are mer-marketing. Once a year, we take a vacation, and proceeding from the sea depths up a strange river, we came out upon this shore. Perhaps you, Sir, will be able to tell us where we are?"

"You are in the Munchkin Country of the Land of Oz," explained the Scarecrow politely. "It is a charming place for a vacation. I would show you about myself if I were not bound on an important mission." Here the Scarecrow sighed deeply.

"Have you a family?" he asked the A-B-Sea Serpent curiously.

"Yes, indeed," replied the monster, snapping its tape-measure tongue in and out, "I have five great-grandmothers, twenty-one grandnieces, seven brothers, and six sisters-in-law!"

"Ah!" murmured the Scarecrow, clasping his hands tragically, "How I envy you. I have no one — no aunts — no ancestors — no family — no family tree but a bean pole. I am, alas, a man without a *past*!" The Scarecrow looked so dejected that the Rattlesnake thought he was going to cry.

"Oh, cheer up!" it begged in a distressed voice. "Think of your *presence* — here — I give you permission to shake me!" The Scarecrow was so affected by this kind offer that he cheered up immediately.

"No past but a presence — I'll remember that!" He swelled out his straw chest complacently, and leaning over, stroked the Rattlesnake on the head.

"Are you good at riddles?" asked the Rattlesnake timidly.

"Well," answered the Scarecrow judiciously, "I have very good brains, given me by the famous Wizard of Oz."

"Then why is the A-B-Sea Serpent like a city?" asked the Rattlesnake promptly.

The Scarecrow thought hard for several seconds.

"Because it is made up of blocks!" he roared triumphantly. "That's easy; now it's my turn. Why is the A-B-Sea Serpent such a slow talker?"

"Give it up!" said the Rattlesnake after shaking himself several times.

"Because his tongue is a tape measure, and he has to measure his words!" cried the Scarecrow, snapping his clumsy fingers. "And that's a good one, if I did make it myself. I must remember to tell it to Dorothy!"

Then he sobered quite suddenly, for the thought of Dorothy brought back the purpose of his journey. Interrupting the Rattlesnake in the midst of a new riddle, he explained how anxious he was to return to the little farm where he had been discovered and try to find some traces of his family.

"And the real riddle," he sighed with a wave of his hand, "is how to cross this river."

"That's easy and no riddle at all," rumbled the A-B-Sea Serpent, who had been listening attentively to the Scarecrow's remarks. "I'll stretch across, and you can walk over." Suiting the action to the word, he began backing very cautiously toward the river so as not to shake the Scarecrow off his feet.

"Mind your P's and Q's!" called the Rattlesnake warningly. It was well that he spoke, for the A-B-Sea Serpent had doubled the P and Q blocks under, and they were ready to snap off. Finally, however, he managed to make a bridge of himself, and the Scarecrow stepped easily over the blocks, the huge serpent holding himself rigid. Just as he reached Y, the unfortunate creature sneezed, and all the blocks rattled together. Up flew the Scarecrow and escaped falling into the stream only by the narrowest margin.

"Blockhead!" shrilled the Rattlesnake, who had taken a great fancy to the Scarecrow.

"I'm all right," cried the Scarecrow rather breathlessly. "Thank you very much!" He sprang nimbly up the bank. "Hope you have a pleasant vacation!"

"Can't, with a rattlepate like that." The A-B-Sea Serpent nodded glumly in the Rattlesnake's direction.

"Now don't quarrel," begged the Scarecrow. "You are both charming and unusual, and if you follow that Yellow Road, you will come to the Emerald City, and Ozma will be delighted to welcome you."

"The Emerald City! We must see that, my dear Rattles." Forgetting his momentary displeasure, the A-B-Sea Serpent pulled himself out of the river, and waving his X Y Z blocks in farewell to the Scarecrow, went clattering down the road, the little Rattlesnake rattling along behind him.

As for the Scarecrow, he continued his journey, and the day was so delightful and the country so pleasant that he almost forgot he had no family. He was treated everywhere with the greatest courtesy and had innumerable invitations from the hospitable Munchkins. He was anxious to reach his destination, however, so he refused them all, and traveling night and day came without further mishap or adventure late on the second evening to the little Munchkin farm where Dorothy had first discovered him. He was curious to know whether the pole on which he had been hoisted to scare away the crows still stood in the cornfield and whether the farmer who had made him could tell him anything further about his history.

"It is a shame to waken him," thought the kind Scarecrow. "I'll just take a look in the cornfield." The moon shone so brightly that he had no trouble finding his way about. With a little cry of pleasure, he pushed his way through the dry cornstalks. There in the centre of the field stood a tall pole — the very identical bean pole from which he had descended.

"All the family or family tree I've got!" cried the Scarecrow, running toward it with emotion.

"What's that?" A window in the farmhouse was thrown up, and a sleepy Munchkin thrust out his head. "What are you doing?" he called crossly.

"Thinking!" said the Scarecrow, leaning heavily against the bean pole.

"Well, don't do it out loud," snapped the farmer. Then, catching a better view of the Scarecrow, he cried in surprise: "Why, it's you!—Come right in, my dear fellow, and give us the latest news from the Emerald City. I'll fetch a candle!"

The farmer was very proud of the Scarecrow. He had made him long ago by stuffing one of his old suits with straw, painting a jolly face on a sack, stuffing that, and fastening the two together. Red boots, a hat, and yellow gloves had finished his man — and nothing could have been jollier than the result. Later on, when the Scarecrow had run off with Dorothy and got his brains from the Wizard of Oz and become ruler of the Emerald City, the little farmer had felt highly gratified.

The Scarecrow, however, was not in a humour for conversation. He wanted to think in peace. "Don't bother!" he called up. "I'm going to spend the night here. I'll see you in the morning."

"All right! Take care of yourself," yawned the farmer, and drew in his head.

For a long time the Scarecrow stood perfectly still beside the bean pole— thinking. Then he got a spade from the shed and began clearing away the cornstalks and dried leaves from around the base of the pole. It was slow work, for his fingers were clumsy, but he persevered. Then a wonderful idea came to him.

"Perhaps if I dig down a bit, I may discover—" He got no further, for at the word "discover," he pushed the spade down with all his might. There was a loud crash. The bottom dropped out of things, and the Scarecrow fell through.

"Great cornstalks!" cried the Scarecrow, throwing up his arms. To his surprise, they came in contact with a stout pole, which he embraced. It was a lifesaver, for he was shooting down into the darkness at a great rate.

"Why!" he gasped as soon as he regained his breath, for he was falling at a terrific rate of speed, "Why, I believe I'm sliding down the *bean pole*!"

Chapter 3

Down the Magic Bean Pole

Hugging the bean pole for dear life, the Scarecrow slid rapidly downward, Everything was dark, but at times a confused roaring sounded in his ears.

"Father, I hear something falling past!" shouted a gruff voice all at once.

"Then reach out and pull it in," growled a still deeper voice. There was a flash of light, a door opened suddenly, and a giant hand snatched the air just above the Scarecrow's head.

"It's a good thing I haven't a heart to fail me," murmured the Scarecrow, glancing up fearfully and clinging more tightly to the pole. "Though I fall, I shall not falter. But where under the earth am I falling to?" At that minute, a door opened far below, and someone called up:

"Who are you? Have out your toll and be

ready to salute the Royal Ruler of the Middlings!"

The Scarecrow had learned in the course of his many and strange adventures that it was best to accede to every request that was reasonable or possible. Realizing that unless he answered at once he would fall past his strange questioners, he shouted amiably:

"I am the Scarecrow of Oz, sliding down my family tree!" The words echoed oddly in the narrow passageway, and by the time he reached the word "tree" the Scarecrow could make out two large brown men leaning from a door somewhere below. Next minute he came to a sharp stop. A board had shot out and closed off the passageway. So sudden was the stop that the Scarecrow was tossed violently upward. While he endeavoured to regain his balance, the two Middlings eyed him curiously.

"So this is the kind of thing they grow on top," said one, holding a lantern close to the Scarecrow's head.

"Toll, Toll!" droned the other, holding out a horribly twisted hand.

"One moment, your Royal Middleness!" cried the Scarecrow, backing as far away from the lantern as he could, for with a straw stuffing one cannot be too careful of fire. He felt in his pocket for an emerald he had picked up in the Emerald City a few days before and handed it gingerly to the Muddy monarch.

"Why do you call me Middleness?" the King demanded angrily, taking the emerald.

"Is your kingdom not in the middle of the earth, and are you not royalty? What could be more proper than Royal Middleness?" asked the Scarecrow, flecking the dust from his hat.

Now that he had a better view, he saw that the two were entirely men of mud, and very roughly put together. Dried grass hair stood erect upon each head, and their faces were large and lumpy and had a disconcerting way of changing shape. Indeed, when the King leaned over to examine the Scarecrow, his features were so soft they seemed to run into his cheek, which hung down alarmingly, while his nose turned sideways and lengthened at least an inch!

Muddle pushed the King's nose back and began spreading his cheek into place. Instead of hands and feet, the Middlings had gnarled and twisted roots which curled up in a perfectly terrifying manner. Their teeth were gold, and their eyes shone like small electric lights. They wore stiff coats of dried mud, buttoned clumsily with lumps of coal, and the King had a tall mud crown. Altogether, the Scarecrow thought he had never seen more disagreeable looking creatures.

"What he needs," spluttered the King, fingering the jewel greedily, "is a coat of mud! Shall we pull him in, Muddle?"

"He's very poorly made, your Mudjesty. Can you work, Carescrow?" asked Muddle, thumping him rudely in the chest.

"Scarecrow, if you please!" The Scarecrow drew himself up and spoke with great difficulty. "I can work with my head!" he added proudly.

"Your head!" roared the King. "Did you hear that, Muddle? He works with his head. What's the matter with your hands?" Again the King lunged forward, and this time his face fell on the other side and had bulged enormously before Muddle could pat it into shape. They began whispering excitedly together, but the Scarecrow made no reply, for looking over their shoulder he glimpsed a dark, forbidding cavern lighted only by the flashing red eyes of thousands of Middlings. They appeared to be digging, and above the rattle of the shovels and picks came the hoarse voice of one of them singing the

Middling National Air. Or so the Scarecrow gathered from the words:

"Oh, chop the brown clods as they fall with a thud!
Three croaks for the Middlings, who stick in the Mud.
Oh, mud, rich and wormy! Oh, mud, sweet and
squirmy!
Oh what is so lovely as Mud! Oh what is so lovely as
Mud!
Three croaks for the Middlings, who delve all the day
In their beautiful Kingdom of soft mud and clay!"

The croaks that came at the end of the song were so terrifying that the Scarecrow shivered in spite of himself.

"Ugh! Hardly a place for a pleasant visit!" he gasped, flattening himself against the wall of the passage. Feeling that matters had gone far enough, he repeated in a loud voice:

"I am the Scarecrow of Oz and desire to continue my fall. I have paid my toll and unless your Royal Middleness release me—"

"Might as well drop him—a useless creature!" whispered Muddle, and before the King had time to object, he jerked the board back. "Fall on!" he screeched maliciously, and the Scarecrow shot down into the darkness, the hoarse screams of the two Middlings echoing after him through the gloom.

No use trying to think! The poor Scarecrow bumped and banged from side to side of the passage. It was all he could do to keep hold of the bean pole, so swiftly was he falling.

"A good thing I'm not made of meat like little Dorothy," he wheezed breathlessly. His gloves were getting worn through from friction with the pole, and the rush of air past his ears was so confusing that he gave up all idea of thinking. Even magic brains refuse to work under such conditions. Down—down—down he plunged till he lost all count of time. Down—down—down— hours and hours! Would he never stop? Then suddenly it grew quite light, and he flashed through what appeared to be a hole in the roof of a huge silver palace, whirled down several stories and landed in a heap on the floor of a great hall. In one hand he clutched a small fan, and in the other a parasol that had snapped off the beanstalk just before he reached the palace roof.

Shaken and bent over double though he was, the Scarecrow could see that he had fallen into a company of great magnificence. He had a confused glimpse of silken clad courtiers, embroidered screens, inlaid floors, and flashing silver lanterns, when there was a thundering bang that hurled him halfway to the roof again. Falling to a sitting position and still clinging to the bean pole, he saw two giant kettle drums nearby, still vibrating from the terrible blows they had received.

The company were staring at him solemnly, and as he attempted to rise, they fell prostrate on their faces. Up flew the poor flimsy Scarecrow again, such was the draught, and this time landed on his face. He was beginning to feel terribly annoyed, but before he could open his mouth or stand up, a deep voice boomed:

"He has come!"

"He has come!" shrilled the rest of the company, thumping their heads on the stone floor. The language seemed strange to the Scarecrow, but oddly enough, he could understand it perfectly. Keeping a tight grasp on the bean pole, he gazed at the prostrate assemblage, too astonished to speak. They looked exactly like the pictures of some Chinamen he had seen in one of Dorothy's picture books back in Oz, but instead of being yellow, their skin was a curious grey, and the hair of old and young alike was silver and worn in long, stiff queues. Before he had time to observe any more, an old, old courtier hobbled forward and beckoned imperiously to a page at the door. The page immediately unfurled a huge silk umbrella and, running forward, held it over the Scarecrow's head.

"Welcome home, sublime and noble Ancestor! Welcome, honourable and exalted Sir." The old gentleman made several deep salaams.

"Welcome, immortal and illustrious Ancestor! Welcome, ancient and serene Father!" cried the others, banging their heads hard on the floor—so hard that their queues flew into the air.

"Ancestor! Father!" mumbled the Scarecrow in a puzzled voice. Then, collecting himself somewhat, he made a deep bow, and sweeping off his hat with a truly royal gesture began: "I am indeed honoured—" But he got no farther. The silken clad courtiers sprang to their feet in a frenzy of joy. A dozen seized him bodily and carried him to a great silver throne room.

"The same beautiful voice!" cried the ancient gentleman, clasping his hands in an ecstasy of feeling.

"It is he! The Emperor! The Emperor has returned! Long live the Emperor!" shouted everyone at once. The confusion grew worse and worse.

"Ancestor! Father! Emperor!" The Scarecrow could scarcely believe his ears. "For a fallen man, I am rising like yeast!" he murmured to himself. Half a dozen courtiers had run outdoors to spread the wonderful news, and soon silver gongs and bells began ringing all over the kingdom, and cries of "The Emperor! The Emperor!" added to the general excitement. Holding fast to the sides of the throne and still grasping the little fan and parasol, the Scarecrow sat blinking with embarrassment.

"If they would just stop emperoring, I could ask them who I am," thought the poor Scarecrow. As if in answer to his thoughts, the tottery old nobleman raised his long arm, and at once the hall became absolutely silent.

"Now!" sighed the Scarecrow, leaning forward. "Now I shall hear something of interest."

Chapter 4

Dorothy's Lonely Breakfast

Dorothy, who occupied one of the cosiest apartments in Ozma's palace, wakened the morning after the party with a feeling of great uneasiness.

At breakfast, the Scarecrow was missing. Although he, the Tin Woodman and Scraps did not require food, they always livened up the table with their conversation. Ordinarily Dorothy would have thought nothing of the Scarecrow's absence, but she could not forget his distressed expression when Professor Wogglebug had so rudely remarked on his family tree. The Professor himself had left before breakfast, and everybody but Dorothy had forgotten all about the Royal Book of Oz.

Already many of Ozma's guests who did not live in the palace were preparing to depart, but Dorothy could not get over her feeling of uneasiness.

The Scarecrow was her very best friend, and it was not like him to go without saying goodbye. So she hunted through the gardens and in every room of the palace and questioned all the servants. Unfortunately, Jellia Jamb, who was the only one who had seen the Scarecrow go, was with her mistress. Ozma always breakfasted alone and spent the morning over state matters. Knowing how busy she was, Dorothy did not like to disturb her. Betsy Bobbin and Trot, real little girls like Dorothy, also lived in the Fairy palace, and Ozma was a great chum for them. But the Kingdom of Oz had to be governed in between times, and they all knew that unless Ozma had the mornings to herself, she could not play with them in the afternoons. So Dorothy searched by herself.

"Perhaps I didn't look hard enough," thought the little girl, and searched the palace all over again.

"Don't worry," advised the Tin Woodman, who was playing checkers with Scraps. "He's probably gone home."

> "He is a man of brains; why worry
> Because he's left us in a hurry?"

chuckled Scraps with a careless wave of her hand,

and Dorothy, laughing in spite of herself, ran out to have another look in the garden.

"That is just what he has done, and if I hurry, I may overtake him. Anyway, I believe I'll go and pay him a visit," thought Dorothy.

Trot and Betsy Bobbin were swinging in one of the royal hammocks, and when Dorothy invited them to go along, they explained that they were going on a picnic with the Tin Woodman. So without waiting to ask anyone else or even whistling for Toto, her little dog, Dorothy skipped out of the garden.

The Cowardly Lion, half asleep under a rose bush, caught a glimpse of her blue dress flashing by, and bounding to his feet thudded after her.

"Where are you going?" he asked, stifling a giant yawn.

"To visit the Scarecrow," explained Dorothy. "He looked so unhappy last night. I am afraid he is worrying about his family tree, and I thought p'raps I could cheer him up."

The Cowardly Lion stretched luxuriously. "I'll go too," he rumbled, giving himself a shake. "But it's the first time I ever heard of the Scarecrow worrying."

"But you see," Dorothy said gently, "Professor

Wogglebug told him he had no family."

"Family! Family fiddlesticks! Hasn't he got us?" The Cowardly Lion stopped and waved his tail indignantly.

"Why, you dear old thing!" Dorothy threw her arms around his neck. "You've given me a lovely idea!"

The Cowardly Lion tried not to look pleased.

"Well, as long as I've given it to you, you might tell me what it is," he suggested mildly.

"Why," said Dorothy, skipping along happily, "we'll let him adopt us and be his really relations. I'll be his sister, and you'll be—"

"His cousin—that is, if you think he wouldn't mind having a great coward like me for a cousin," finished the Cowardly Lion in an anxious voice.

"Do you still feel as cowardly as ever?" asked Dorothy sympathetically.

"More so!" sighed the great beast, glancing apprehensively over his shoulder. This made Dorothy laugh, for although the lion trembled like a jelly at the approach of danger, he always managed to fight with great valour, and the little girl felt safer with him than with the whole army of Oz, who never were frightened but who always ran away.

Now anyone who is at all familiar with his Geozify knows that the Fairyland of Oz is divided into four parts, exactly like a parchesi board, with the Emerald City in the very centre, the purple Gillikin Country to the north, the red Quadling Country to the south, the blue Munchkin Country to the east, and the yellow Country of the Winkies to the west. It was toward the west that Dorothy and the Cowardly Lion turned their steps, for it was in the Winkie Country that the Scarecrow had built his gorgeous golden tower in exactly the shape of a huge ear of corn.

Dorothy ran along beside the Cowardly Lion, chatting over their many adventures in Oz, and stopping now and then to pick buttercups and daisies that dotted the roadside. She tied a big bunch to the tip of her friend's tail and twined some more in his mane, so that he presented a very festive appearance indeed. Then, when she grew tired, she climbed on his big back, and swiftly they jogged through the pleasant land of the Winkies. The people waved to them from windows and fields, for everyone loved little Dorothy and the big lion, and as they passed a neat yellow cottage, a little Winkie Lady came running down the path with a cup of tea in one hand

and a bucket in the other.

"I saw you coming and thought you might be thirsty," she called hospitably. Dorothy drank her cup without alighting.

"We're in an awful hurry; we're visiting the Scarecrow," she exclaimed apologetically. The lion drank his bucket of tea at one gulp. It was so hot that it made his eyes water.

"How I loathe tea! If I hadn't been such a coward, I'd have upset the bucket," groaned the lion as the little Winkie Lady went back into her house. "But no, I was afraid of hurting her feelings. Ugh, what a terrible thing it is to be a coward!"

"Nonsense!" said Dorothy, wiping her eyes with her handkerchief. "You're not a coward, you're just polite. But let's run very fast so we can reach the Scarecrow's in time for lunch."

So like the wind away raced the Cowardly Lion, Dorothy holding fast to his mane, with her curls blowing straight out behind, and in exactly two Oz hours and seventeen Winkie minutes they came to the dazzling corn-ear residence of their old friend. Hurrying through the cornfields that surrounded his singular mansion, Dorothy and the Cowardly Lion rushed through the open door.

"We've come for lunch," announced Dorothy.

"And I'm hungry enough to eat crow," rumbled the lion. Then both stopped in dismay, for the big reception room was empty. From a room above came a shuffling of feet, and Blink, the Scarecrow's gentlemanly housekeeper, came running down the stairs.

"Where's the Scarecrow?" asked Dorothy anxiously. "Isn't he here?"

"Here! Isn't he there? Isn't he in the Emerald City?" gasped the little Winkie, putting his specs on upside down.

"No—at least, I don't think so. Oh, dear, I just felt that something had happened to him!" wailed Dorothy, sinking into an ebony armchair and fanning herself with a silk sofa cushion.

"Now don't be alarmed." The Cowardly Lion rushed to Dorothy's side and knocked three vases and a clock off a little table, just to show how calm he was. "Think of his brains! The Scarecrow has never come to harm yet, and all we have to do is to return to the Emerald City and look in Ozma's Magic Picture. Then, when we know where he is, we can go and find him and tell him about our little adoption plan," he added, looking hopefully at Dorothy.

"The Scarecrow himself couldn't have spoken more sensibly," observed Blink with a great sigh of relief, and even Dorothy felt better.

In Ozma's palace, as many of you know, there is a Magic Picture, and when Ozma or Dorothy want to see any of their friends, they have merely to wish to see them, and instantly the picture shows the person wished for and exactly what he is doing at that certain time.

"Of course!" sighed Dorothy. "Why didn't I think of it myself?"

"Better have some lunch before you start back," suggested Blink, and bustling about had soon set out an appetizing repast. Dorothy was too busy worrying about the Scarecrow to have much appetite, but the Cowardly Lion swallowed seventeen roasts and a bucket of corn syrup.

"To give me courage!" he explained to Dorothy, licking his chops. "There's nothing that makes me so cowardly as an empty stomach!"

It was quite late in the afternoon before they could get away. Blink insisted on putting up a lunch, and it took some time to make enough sandwiches for the Cowardly Lion. But at last it was ready and packed into an old hat box belonging to Mops, the

Scarecrow's cook. Then Dorothy, balancing the box carefully on her lap, climbed on the Cowardly Lion's back, and assuring Blink that they would return in a few days with his master, they bade him farewell. Blink almost spoiled things by bursting into tears, but he managed to restrain himself long enough to say goodbye and Dorothy and the Cowardly Lion, feeling a little solemn themselves, started toward the Emerald City.

"My, but it's growing dark," said Dorothy after they had gone several miles. "I believe it's going to storm."

Scarcely had she finished speaking before there was a terrific crash of thunder. The Cowardly Lion promptly sat down. Off of his back bounced the sandwich box and into the sandwich box rolled Dorothy, head first.

"How terribly upsetting," coughed the Cowardly Lion.

"I should say it was!" Dorothy crawled indignantly out of the hat box and began wiping the butter from her nose. "You've simply ruined the supper!"

"It was my heart," explained the Cowardly Lion sorrowfully. "It jumped so hard that it upset me, but climb on my back again, and I'll run very fast to some place of shelter."

"But where are you?" Dorothy asked in real alarm, for it had grown absolutely dark.

"Here," quavered the Cowardly Lion, and guided by his voice, Dorothy stumbled over to him and climbed again on his back. One crash of thunder followed another, and at each crash the Cowardly Lion leapt forward a bit faster until they fairly flew through the dark.

"It won't take us long to reach the Emerald City at this rate!" called Dorothy, but the wind tossed the words far behind her, and seeing that conversation was impossible, she clung fast to the lion's mane and began thinking about the Scarecrow. The thunder continued at frequent intervals, but there was no rain, and after they had been running for what seemed to Dorothy hours and hours, a sudden terrific bump sent her flying over the lion's head into a bush. Too breathless to speak, she felt herself carefully all over. Then, finding that she was still in one piece, she called to the Cowardly Lion. She could hear him moaning and muttering about his heart.

"Any bones broken?" she asked anxiously.

"Only my head," groaned the lion dismally. Just then the darkness lifted as suddenly as it had fallen, and Dorothy saw him leaning against a tree with his eyes closed. There was a big bump on his head. With a little cry of sympathy, Dorothy hurried toward him, when all at once something strange about their surroundings struck her.

"Why, where are we?" cried the little girl, stopping short. The lion's eyes flew open, and forgetting all about his bump, he looked around in dismay. No sign of the Emerald City anywhere. Indeed, they were in a great, dim forest, and considering the number of trees, it is a wonder that they had not run into one long ago.

"I must have run the wrong way," faltered the Cowardly Lion in a distressed voice.

"You couldn't help that; anyone would lose his way in the dark," said Dorothy generously. "But I wish we hadn't fallen in the sandwiches. I'm hungry!"

"So am I. Do you think anyone lives in this forest, Dorothy?"

Dorothy did not answer, for just then she caught sight of a big sign nailed to one of the trees.

"Turn to the right," directed the sign.

"Oh, come on!" cried Dorothy, cheering up

immediately. "I believe we're going to have another adventure."

"I'd rather have some supper," sighed the Cowardly Lion wistfully, "but unless we want to spend the night here, we might as well move along. I'm to be fed up on adventure, I suppose."

"Turn to the left," advised the next sign, and the two turned obediently and hurried on, trying to keep a straight course through the trees. In a Fairyland like Oz, where there are no trains or trolleys or even horses for traveling ('cepting Ozma's sawhorse), there are bound to be unexplored portions. And though Dorothy had been at one time or another in almost every part of Oz, the country through which they were now passing was totally unfamiliar to her. Night was coming on, and it was growing so dark that she could hardly read the third sign when they presently came upon it.

"Don't sing," directed the sign sternly.

"Sing!" snapped Dorothy indignantly, "Who wants to sing?"

"We might as well keep to the left," said the Cowardly Lion in a resigned voice, and they walked along for some time in silence. The trees were thinning out, and as they came to the edge of the forest, another sign confronted them.

"Slow down," read Dorothy with great difficulty. "What nonsense! If we slow down, how shall we ever get anywhere?"

"Wait a minute," mused the Cowardly Lion, half closing his eyes. "Aren't there two roads just ahead, one going up and one going down? We're to take the down road, I suppose. 'Slow down,' isn't that what it says?"

Slow down it surely was, for the road was so steep and full of stones that Dorothy and the Cowardly Lion had to pick their way with utmost care. But even bad roads must end somewhere, and coming suddenly to the edge of the woods, they saw a great city lying just below. A dim light burned over the main gate, and toward this the Cowardly Lion and Dorothy hurried as fast as they could. This was not very fast, for an unaccountable drowsiness was stealing over them.

Slowly and more slowly, the tired little girl and her great four-footed companion advanced toward the dimly lighted gate. They were so drowsy that they had ceased to talk. But they dragged on.

"Hah, hoh, hum!" yawned the Cowardly Lion. "What makes my feet so heavy?"

He stopped short and examined each of his four feet sleepily.

Dorothy swallowed a yawn and tried to run, but a walk was all she could manage.

"Hah, hoh, hum!" she gaped, stumbling along with her eyes closed.

By the time they had reached the gate, they were yawning so hard that the Cowardly Lion had nearly dislocated his jaw, and Dorothy was perfectly breathless. Holding to the lion's mane to steady herself, Dorothy blinked up uncertainly at the sign over the gate.

"Hah—here we are—Hoh!" She held her hand wearily before her mouth.

Then, with a great effort, she read the words of the sign.

"Um—Great—Grand and Mighty Slow Kingdom of Pokes! Uh-hah—Pokes! Do you hear? Hah, hoh, hu, uum!"

Dorothy looked about in alarm, despite her sleepiness.

"Do you hear?" she repeated anxiously as no answer came through the gloom.

The Cowardly Lion did not hear. He had fallen down and was fast asleep, and so in another minute was Dorothy, her head pillowed against his kind, comfortable, cowardly heart. Fast asleep at the gates of a strange grey city!

Chapter 5

Sir Hokus of Pokes

It was long past sun-up before Dorothy awoke. She rubbed her eyes, yawned once or twice, and then shook the Cowardly Lion. The gates of the city were open, and although it looked even greyer in the daytime than it looked at night, the travellers were too hungry to be particular. A large placard was posted just inside:

THIS IS POKES!
DON'T RUN!
DON'T SING!
TALK SLOWLY!
DON'T WHISTLE!
Order of the Chief Poker.

read Dorothy. "How cheerful! Hah, hoh, hum-mm!"

"Don't!" begged the Cowardly Lion with tears in his eyes. "If I yawn again, I'll swallow my tail, and if I don't have something to eat soon, I'll do it anyway. Let's hurry! There's something queer about this place, Dorothy! Ah, hah, hoh, hum-mm!"

Stifling their yawns, the two started down the long, narrow street. The houses were of grey stone, tall and stiff with tiny barred windows. It was absolutely quiet, and not a person was in sight. But when they turned the corner, they saw a crowd of queer-looking people creeping toward them. These singular individuals stopped between each step and stood perfectly still, and Dorothy was so surprised at their unusual appearance that she laughed right in the middle of a yawn.

In the first place, they never lifted their feet, but pushed them along like skates. The women were dressed in grey polka-dot dresses with huge poke bonnets that almost hid their fat, sleepy, wide-mouthed faces. Most of them had pet snails on strings, and so slowly did they move that it looked as though the snails were tugging them along.

The men were dressed like a party of congressmen, but instead of high hats wore large red nightcaps, and they were all as solemn as owls. It seemed impossible for them to keep both eyes open at the same time, and at first Dorothy thought they were winking at her. But as the whole company continued to stare fixedly with one open eye, she burst out laughing. At the unexpected sound (for no one had ever laughed in Pokes before), the women picked up their snails in a great fright, and the men clapped their fingers to their ears or to the places where their ears were under the red nightcaps.

"These must be the Slow Pokes," giggled Dorothy, nudging the Cowardly Lion. "Let's go to meet them, for they'll never reach us at the rate they are coming!"

"There's something wrong with my feet," rumbled the Cowardly Lion without looking up. "Hah, hoh, hum! What's the use of hurrying?" The fact of the matter was that they couldn't hurry if they tried. Indeed, they could hardly lift their feet at all.

"I wish the Scarecrow were with us," sighed the Cowardly Lion, shuffling along unhappily. "He never grows sleepy, and he always knows what to do."

"No use wishing," yawned Dorothy. "I only hope he's not as lost as we are."

By struggling hard, they just managed to keep moving, and by the time they came up with the Slow Pokes, they were completely worn out. A cross-looking Poke held up his arm threateningly, and Dorothy and the Cowardly Lion stopped.

"You—" said the Poke; then closed his mouth and stood staring vacantly for a whole minute.

"Are—" He brought out the word with a perfectly enormous yawn, and Dorothy began fanning the Cowardly Lion with her hat, for he showed signs of falling asleep again.

"What?" she asked crossly.

"Under—" sighed the Poke after a long pause, and Dorothy, seeing that there was no hurrying him, began counting to herself. Just as she reached sixty, the Poke pushed back his red nightcap and shouted:

"Arrest!"

"Arrest!" shouted all the other Pokes so loud that the Cowardly Lion roused himself with a start, and the pet snails stuck out their heads. "A rest? A rest is not what we want! We want breakfast!" growled the lion irritably and started to roar, but a yawn spoiled it. (One simply cannot look fierce by yawning.)

"You—" began the Poke. But Dorothy could not stand hearing the same slow speech again. Putting her fingers in her ears, she shouted back:

"What for?"

The Pokes regarded her sternly. Some even opened both eyes. Then the one who had first addressed the, covering a terrific gape with one hand, pointed with the other to a sign on a large post at the corner of the street.

"Speed limit 1/4 mile an hour" said the sign.

"We're arrested for speeding!" shouted Dorothy in the Cowardly Lion's ear.

"Did you say feeding?" asked the poor lion, waking up with a start. "If I go to sleep again before I'm fed, I'll starve to death!"

"Then keep awake," yawned Dorothy. By this time, the Pokes had surrounded them and were waving them imperiously ahead. They looked so threatening that Dorothy and the Cowardly Lion began to creep in the direction of a gloomy, grey castle. Of the journey neither of them remembered a thing, for with the gaping and yawning Pokes it was almost impossible to keep awake. But they must have walked in their sleep, for the next thing Dorothy knew, a harsh voice called slowly:

"Poke—him!"

Greatly alarmed, Dorothy opened her eyes. They were in a huge stone hall hung all over with rusty armour, and seated on a great stone chair, snoring so loudly that all the steel helmets rattled, was a Knight. The tallest and crossest of the Pokes rushed at him with a long poker, giving him such a shove that he sprawled to the floor.

"So—" yawned the Cowardly Lion, awakened by the clatter, "Knight has fallen!"

"Prisoners—Sir Hokus!" shouted the Chief Poker, lifting the Knight's plume and speaking into the helmet as if he were telephoning.

The Knight arose with great dignity, and after straightening his armour, let down his visor, and Dorothy saw a kind, timid face with melancholy blue eyes—not at all Pokish, as she explained to Ozma later.

"What means this unwonted clamour?" asked Sir Hokus, peering curiously at the prisoners.

"We're sorry to waken you," said Dorothy politely, "but could you please give us some breakfast?"

"A lot!" added the Cowardly Lion, licking his chops.

"It's safer for me to sing," said the Knight mournfully, and throwing back his head, he roared in a high, hoarse voice:

"Don't yawn! Don't yawn!
We're out of breath—

Begone—BEGONE
Or die the death!"

The Cowardly Lion growled threateningly and began lashing his tail.

"If he weren't in a can, I'd eat him," he rumbled, "but I never could abide tinned meat."

"He's not in a can, he's in armour," explained Dorothy, too interested to pay much attention to the Cowardly Lion, for at the first note of the Knight's song, the Pokes began scowling horribly, and by the time he had finished they were backing out of the room faster than Dorothy ever imagined they could go.

"So that's why the sign said don't sing," thought Dorothy to herself. The air seemed clearer somehow, and she no longer felt sleepy.

When the last Poke had disappeared, the Knight sighed and climbed gravely back on his stone chair.

"My singing makes them very wroth. In faith, they cannot endure music; it wakens them," explained Sir Hokus. "But hold, 'twas food you asked of me. Breakfast, I believe you called it." With an uneasy glance at the Cowardly Lion, who was sniffing the air hungrily, the Knight banged on his steel armour with his sword, and a fat, lazy Poke shuffled slowly into the hall.

"Pid, bring the stew," roared Sir Hokus as the Poke stood blinking at them dully.

"Stew, Pid!" he repeated loudly, and began to hum under his breath, at which Pid fairly ran out of the room, returning in a few minutes with a large yellow bowl. This he handed ungraciously to Dorothy. Then he brought a great copper tub of the stuff for the Cowardly Lion and retired sulkily.

Dorothy thought she had never tasted anything more delicious. The Cowardly Lion was gulping down his share with closed eyes, and both, I am very sorry to say, forgot even to thank Sir Hokus.

"Are you perchance a damsel in distress?"

Quite startled, Dorothy looked up from her bowl and saw the Knight regarding her wistfully.

"She's in Pokes, and that's the same thing," said the Cowardly Lion without opening his eyes.

"We're lost," began the little girl, "but—"

There was something so quaint and gentle about the Knight, that she soon found herself talking to him like an old friend. She told him all of their adventures since leaving the Emerald City and even told about the disappearance of the Scarecrow.

"Passing strange, yet how refreshing," murmured Sir Hokus. "And if I seem a little behind times, you must not blame me. For centuries, I have dozed in this grey castle, and it cometh over me that things have greatly changed. This beast now, he talks quite manfully, and this Kingdom that you mention, this Oz? Never heard of it!"

"Never heard of Oz?" gasped the little girl. "Why, you're a subject of Oz, and Pokes is in Oz, though I don't know just where."

Here Dorothy gave him a short history of the Fairy country, and of the many adventures she had had since she had come there. Sir Hokus listened with growing melancholy.

"To think," he sighed mournfully, "that I was prisoner here while all that was happening!"

"Are you a prisoner?" asked Dorothy in surprise. "I thought you were King of the Pokes!"

"Uds daggers!" thundered Sir Hokus so suddenly that Dorothy jumped. "I am a knight!"

Seeing her startled expression, he controlled himself. "I was a knight," he continued brokenly. "Long centuries ago, mounted on my goodly steed, I fared from my father's castle to offer my sword to a mighty king. His name?" Sir Hokus tapped his forehead uncertainly. "Go to, I have forgot."

"Could it have been King Arthur?" exclaimed Dorothy, wide-eyed with interest. "Why, just think of your being still alive!"

"That's just the point," choked the Knight. "I've been alive—still, so still that I've forgotten everything. Why, I can't even remember how I used to talk," he confessed miserably.

"But how did you get here?" rumbled the Cowardly Lion, who did not like being left out of the conversation.

"I had barely left my father's castle before I met a stranger," said Sir Hokus, sitting up very straight, "who challenged me to battle. I spurred my horse forward, our lances met, and the stranger was unseated. But by my faith, 'twas no mortal Knight." Sir Hokus sighed deeply and lapsed into silence.

"What happened?" asked Dorothy curiously, for Sir Hokus seemed to have forgotten them.

"The Knight," said he with another mighty sigh, "struck the ground with his lance and cried, 'Live Wretch, for centuries in the stupidest country out of the world,' and disappeared. And here—here I am!" With a despairing gesture, Sir Hokus arose, big tears splashing down his armour.

"I feel that I am brave, very brave, but how am I to know until I have encountered danger? Ah, friends, behold in me a Knight who has never had a real adventure, never killed a dragon, nor championed a Lady, nor gone on a Quest!"

Dropping on his knees before the little girl, Sir Hokus took her hand.

"Let me go with you on this Quest for the valiant Scarecrow. Let me be your good Night!" he begged eagerly.

"Good night," coughed the Cowardly Lion, who, to tell the truth, was feeling a bit jealous. But Dorothy was thrilled, and as Sir Hokus continued to look at her pleadingly, she took off her hair ribbon and bound it 'round his arm.

"You shall be my own true Knight, and I your Lady Fair!" she announced solemnly, and exactly as she had read in books.

At this interesting juncture the Cowardly Lion gave a tremendous yawn, and Sir Hokus with an exclamation of alarm jumped to his feet. The Pokes had returned to the hall, and Dorothy felt herself falling asleep again.

"Up, up, my lieges and away!
We take the field again—
For Ladies fair we fight today
And KING! Up, up, my merry men!"

shrilled the Knight as if he were leading an army to battle. The Pokes opened both eyes, but did not immediately retire. Sir Hokus bravely swallowed a yawn and hastily clearing his throat shouted another song, which he evidently made up on the spur of the moment:

"Avaunt! Be off! Be gone – Methinks
We'll be asleep in forty winks!"

This time the Pokes left sullenly, but the effect of their presence had thrown Dorothy, the Cowardly Lion, and the Knight into a violent fit of the gapes.

"If I fall asleep, nothing can save you," said Sir Hokus in an agitated voice. "Hah, hoh, hum! Hah—!"

The Knight's eyes closed.

"Don't do it, don't do it!" begged Dorothy, shaking him violently. "Can't we run away?"

"I've been trying for five centuries," wailed

the Knight in a discouraged voice, "but I always fall asleep before I reach the gate, and they bring me back here. They're rather fond of me in their slow way," he added apologetically.

"Couldn't you keep singing?" asked the Cowardly Lion anxiously, for the prospect of a five-century stay in Pokes was more than he could bear.

"Couldn't we all sing?" suggested Dorothy. "Surely all three of us won't fall asleep at once."

"I'm not much of a singer," groaned the Cowardly Lion, beginning to tremble, "but I'm willing to do my share!"

"I like you," said Sir Hokus, going over and thumping the Cowardly Lion approvingly on the back. "You ought to be knighted!"

The lion blinked his eyes, for Sir Hokus' iron fist bruised him severely, but knowing it was kindly meant, he bore it bravely.

"I am henceforth a beknighted lion," he whispered to Dorothy while Sir Hokus was straightening his armour. Next the Knight took down an iron poker, which he handed to Dorothy.

"To wake us up with," he explained. "And now, Lady Dorothy, if you are ready, we will start on the Quest for the honourable Scarecrow, and remember, everybody sing— *Sing for your life!*"

Chapter 6

Singing Their Way Out of Pokes

Taking a deep breath, Sir Hokus, the Cowardly Lion and Dorothy burst out of the hall singing at the top of their voices.

"Three blind mice—!" sang Dorothy.

"Across the plain!" shouted Sir Hokus.

"I am the Cowardly Lion of Oz!" roared the lion.

The Pokes were so taken aback at the horrid sounds that they ran scurrying right and left. In another minute the three were out of the castle and singing their way through the gloomy garden. Dorothy stuck to the "Three Blind Mice". Sir Hokus sang verse after verse of an old English ballad, and the Cowardly Lion roared and gurgled a song of his own making, which, considering it was a first attempt, was not so bad:

"I am the Cowardly Lion of Oz!
Be good! Begone! Beware! Becoz
When I am scared full fierce I be;
Br—rah—grr—ruff, look out for me!"

The Pokes stumbled this way and that, and all went well until they rushed into a company of Pokes who were playing croquet. The slowness with which they raised their mallets fascinated Dorothy, and she stopped to watch them in spite of herself.

"Don't stop! Sing!" growled the Cowardly Lion in the middle of a line.

To make up for lost time, Dorothy closed her eyes and sang harder than ever, but alas! next instant she fell over a wicket, which so deprived her of breath that she could barely scramble up, let alone sing. As soon as she stopped singing, the Pokes paused in their flight, and as soon as they paused Dorothy began to gape. Singing for dear life, Sir Hokus jerked Dorothy by the arm, and the Cowardly Lion roared so loud that the Pokes covered their ears and began backing away.

"There was a Knight! Come on, come on!" sang Sir Hokus, and Dorothy came, and in a few minutes was able to take up the "Three Blind Mice" again. But running and singing at the same time is not an easy task. And running through Pokes is like trying to run through water. (You know how hard that is?)

"Three Blind Mice—uh—hah—Three Blind— Mice—uh-hah—I can't sing another note! Thu—ree—!" gasped poor Dorothy, stumbling along, while the Cowardly Lion was puffing like an engine. The Pokes in the garden had recovered from their first alarm and were following at a safe distance. The gates of the city were only a short distance off, but it seemed to Dorothy that she could not go another step.

A large group of Pokes had gathered at the gates, and unless they could sing their way through, they would fall asleep and be carried ignominiously back to the castle.

"Now!" wheezed Sir Hokus, "Remember, it is for the Scarecrow!" All of them swallowed, took a deep breath, and put their last remaining strength into their voices. But a wily Poke who had stuffed some cotton in his ears now approached pushing a little cart.

"Take—!" he drawled, and before Dorothy realized what she was doing, she had accepted a cone from the Poke.

"Hah, hoh, hum! Why, it's hokey pokey!" spluttered Dorothy, and with a deep sigh of delight she took a large bite of the pink ice cream. How cool it felt on her dry throat! She opened her mouth for a second taste, yawned terrifically, and fell with a thud to the stone pavement.

"Dorothy!" wailed Sir Hokus, stopping short in his song and bending over the little girl. The poor Cowardly Lion gave a gulp of despair and began running around the two, roaring and singing in a choked voice. The Pokes nodded to each other in a pleased fashion, and the Chief Poker started cautiously toward them with a long, thick rope. The Cowardly Lion redoubled his efforts. Then, seeing Sir Hokus about to fall, he jumped on the Knight with all his strength. Down crashed Sir Hokus, his armour clanging against the stones that paved the gateway.

"Sing!" roared the Cowardly Lion, glaring at him fiercely. The fall wakened the poor Knight, but he had not the strength to rise. Sitting on the hard stones and looking reproachfully at the Cowardly Lion, he began his ballad in a half-hearted fashion. The Cowardly Lion's heart was like to burst between lack of breath and fear, but making one last tremendous effort and still roaring his song, he bounded at the Chief Poker, seized the rope, and was back before the stupid creature had time to yawn.

"Tie it around your waist; take Dorothy in your arms!" gasped the Cowardly Lion out of the corner of his mouth. Sir Hokus, though completely dazed, had just enough presence of mind to obey, and the next minute the Cowardly Lion, growling between his teeth like a good fellow, was dashing through the group of Pokes, the other end of the rope in his mouth.

Bumpety bump—bump—bump! Bangety-bang-bang! went Sir Hokus over the cobbles, holding his helmet with one hand and Dorothy fast in the other arm. The Pokes fell this way and that, and such was the determination of the Cowardly Lion that he never stopped till he was out of the gate and halfway up the rough road they had so recently travelled. Then with a mighty sigh, he dropped the rope, rolled over and over down the hill, and lay panting with exhaustion at the bottom.

The bumping over the cobbles had wakened Sir Hokus thoroughly. Indeed, the poor Knight was black and blue, and his armour dented and scraped frightfully in important places.

Dorothy, considerably shaken, opened her eyes and began feebly singing "Three Blind Mice."

"No need," puffed Sir Hokus, lifting her off his lap and rising stiffly.

"Yon noble beast has rescued us."

"Won't the Pokes come up here?" asked Dorothy, staring around a bit dizzily.

"They cannot live out of the kingdom," said the Knight, and Dorothy drew a big sigh of relief. Sir Hokus, however, was looking very grave.

"I have failed on my first adventure. Had it not been for the Cowardly Lion, we would now be prisoners in Pokes," he murmured sadly. Then he unfastened the plume from his helmet. "It beseemeth me not to wear it," sighed the Knight mournfully, and though Dorothy tried her best to comfort him, he refused to put it back. Finally, she fastened the plume to her dress, and they went down to the Cowardly Lion.

There was a little spring nearby, and after they had poured six helmets of water over his head, the lion opened his eyes. "Been in a good many fights," gasped the lion, "but I never fought one like this. Singing, bah!"

"Noble Sir, how can I ever repay you?" faltered the Knight. "Alas, that I have failed in the hour of trial!"

"Why, it wasn't a question of courage at all," rumbled the Cowardly Lion, greatly embarrassed. "I had the loudest voice and the most breath, that's all! You got the rough end of it." Sir Hokus looked ruefully at his armour. The back was entirely squashed.

"Never mind!" said the Knight bravely. "It is the front one presents to the foe."

"Now you're talking like a real Knight," said Dorothy. "A while ago you said, 'Yon' and 'beseemeth,' and first thing you know the talk will all come back to you." Sir Hokus' honest face shone with pleasure.

"Odds bludgeons and truncheons! The little maid is right!" he exclaimed, striking an attitude. "And once it does, the rest will be easy."

"Don't say rest to me," begged the Cowardly Lion, getting slowly to his feet. "Hah, hoh, hum! Just to think of it makes me yawn. Now don't you think we had better start off?"

"If you're rested," began Dorothy. The Cowardly Lion put his paw over his ear and looked so comical that both Dorothy and Sir Hokus laughed heartily.

"If you're ready," amended Dorothy, and the three adventurers started up the steep road. "The first thing to do," said the little girl, "is to get back to the Emerald City as quickly as we can."

At this very minute Glinda, the Good Sorceress of Oz, in her palace in the Quadling Country, was puzzling over an entry in the Magic Record Book. This book tells everything that is happening in the world and out, and while it does not give details, it is a very useful possession.

"The Emperor of the Silver Islands," read Glinda, ""has returned to his people."

"Now who is the Emperor of the Silver Islands?" she asked herself. She puzzled about it for a long while, and then, deciding that it had nothing to do with the Fairy Kingdom of Oz, she closed the book and went for a walk in the palace garden.

Dorothy and Sir Hokus and the Cowardly Lion had meanwhile reached the first sign in the dim forest, the sign directing travellers to Pokes. Two roads branched out through the forest, and after much debating they took the wider.

"Do you 'spose this leads to the Emerald City?" asked Cowardly Lion dubiously.

"Time will tell, time will tell," said Sir Hokus

cheerfully.

"Yes," murmured the Cowardly Lion, "time will tell. But what?"

Chapter 7

The Scarecrow is Hailed as Emperor

L eaning forward on the great throne, the Scarecrow waited impatiently for the ancient gentleman to speak. The grey-skinned courtiers were eyeing him expectantly, and just as the suspense became almost unendurable, the old man threw up his arms and cried sharply:

"The prophecy of the magic beanstalk has been fulfilled. In this radiant and sublime Scarecrowcus, the spirit of Chang Wang Woe, the mighty, has returned. And I, the Grand Chew Chew of the realm, prostrate myself before this wonderful Scarecrowcus, Emperor of the Silver Islands." So, likewise, did all the company present, and the Scarecrow, taken unawares, flew up several feet and landed in a heap on the steps leading to the throne. He climbed back hurriedly, picking up the fan and parasol that he had plucked from the beanstalk.

"I wish Professor Wogglebug could hear this," said the Scarecrow, settling himself complacently. "But I must watch out, and remember to hold on."

The Grand Chew Chew was the first to rise, and folding his arms, he asked solemnly:

"What are your commands, Ancient and Honourable Scarecrowcus?"

"If you'd just omit the Cus," begged the Scarecrow in an embarrassed voice, "I believe I could think better. Am I in China, or where? Are you Chinamen, or what?"

"We are Silvermen," said the Grand Chew Chew impressively, "and a much older race than our Chinese cousins. They are people of the sun. We are people of the stars. Has your Highness so soon forgotten?"

"I am afraid," said the Scarecrow, rubbing his chin reflectively, "that I have." He gazed slowly around the great throne room. Ozma's palace itself was not more dazzling. The floor of dull silver blocks was covered with rich blue rugs. Furniture, chairs, screens and everything were made of silver inlaid with precious stones. Filigreed silver lanterns hung from the high ceilings, and tall silver vases filled with pink and blue blossoms filled the rooms with their perfume. Blue flags embroidered with silver stars fluttered from the walls and the tips of the pikebearers' spears, and silver seemed to be so plentiful that even shoes were fashioned of it. Faintly through the windows came the sweet tones of a hundred silver chimes, and altogether the Scarecrow was quite dazed by his apparent good fortune. Surely they had called him Emperor, but how could that be? He turned to address the Grand Chew Chew; then as he saw out of the corner of his eye that the assemblage were making ready to fall upon their faces, he exclaimed in a hoarse whisper:

"May I speak to you alone?" The Grand Chew Chew waved his hand imperiously, and the courtiers with a great crackling of silver brocade backed from the hall.

"Very kind of them to bow, but I wish they wouldn't," sighed the Scarecrow, sinking back on the great throne. "It blows one about so. I declare, if another person falls at my feet, I'll have nervous prostration."

Again he took a long survey of the hall, then turned to the Grand Chew Chew. "Would you mind," he asked simply, "telling me again who

I am and how?"

"Who and how? Who—You are, illustrious Sir, the Emperor Chang Wang Woe, or to be more exact, his spirit!"

"I have always been a spirited person," observed the Scarecrow dubiously, "but never a spirit without a person. I must insist on being a person."

"How?" the Grand Chew Chew proceeded without noticing the Scarecrow's remarks. "Fifty years ago—after your Extreme Highness had defeated in battle the King of the Golden Islands—a magician entered the realm. This magician, in the employ of this wicked king, entered a room in the palace where your Highness lay sleeping and by an act of necromancy changed you to a crocus!"

"Ouch!" exclaimed the Scarecrow, shuddering involuntarily.

"And had it not been for the Empress, your faithful wife, you would have been lost forever to the Empire."

"Wife?" gasped the Scarecrow faintly. "Have I a wife?"

"If your Highness will permit me to finish," begged the Grand Chew Chew with great dignity.

The Scarecrow nodded.

"Your wife, Tsing Tsing, the beautiful, took the crocus, which was fading rapidly, and planted it in a silver bowl in the centre of this very hall and for three days kept it fresh with her tears. Waking on the third morning, the Empress was amazed to see in place of the crocus a giant bean pole that extended to the roof of the palace and disappeared among the clouds."

"Ah!" murmured the Scarecrow, looking up, "My family tree!"

"Beside the bean pole lay a crumpled parchment." The Grand Chew Chew felt in the sleeve of his kimono and brought out a bit of crumpled silver paper, and adjusting his horn spectacles, read slowly.

"Into the first being who touches this magic pole—on the other side of the world—the spirit of Emperor Chang Wang Woe will enter. And fifty years from this day, he will return—to save his people."

The Grand Chew Chew took off his specs and folded up the paper. "The day has come! You have come down the bean pole, and are undoubtedly that being who has gone from Emperor to crocus to Scarecrowcus. I have ruled the Islands these fifty years; have seen to the education of your sons and grandsons. And now, gracious and exalted Master, as I am an old man I ask you to relieve me from the cares of state."

"Sons! Grandsons!" choked the Scarecrow, beginning to feel very much alarmed indeed. "How old am I?"

"Your Highness," said the Grand Chew Chew with a deep salaam, "is as old as I. In other words, you are in the ripe and glorious eighty-fifth year of your Majesty's illustrious and useful age."

"Eighty five!" gasped the Scarecrow, staring in dismay at the grey, wrinkled face of the old Silverman. "Now see here, Chew Chew, are you sure of that?"

"Quite sure, Immortal and Honoured Master!"

The Scarecrow could not help but be convinced of the truth of the Grand Chew Chew's story. The pole in the Munchkin farmer's cornfield was none other than the magic beanstalk, and he, thrust on the pole by the farmer to scare away the crows, had received the spirit of the Emperor Chang Wang Woe. "Which accounts for my cleverness," he thought gloomily. Now, surely he should have been pleased, for he had come in search of a family, but the acquisition of an empire, sons and grandsons, and old age, all in a trice, fairly took his breath away.

"Does the prophecy say anything about restoring my imperial person?" he asked anxiously, for the thought of looking like Chew Chew was not a cheerful one.

"Alas, no!" sighed the Grand Chew Chew sorrowfully. "But we have very clever wizards on the Island, and I shall set them at work on the problem at once."

"Now don't be in such a rush," begged the Scarecrow, secretly determined to lock up the wizards at the first opportunity. "I'm rather fond of this shape. You see, it requires no food and never grows tired—or old!"

"The royal robes will in a measure conceal it," murmured the Grand Chew Chew politely, and clapped his hands. A little servitor bounced into the hall.

"A royal robe, Quick Silver, for his Radiant Highness," snapped the Grand Chew Chew. In a moment Quick Silver had returned with a magnificent purple satin robe embroidered in silver threads and heavy with jewels, and a hat of silver cloth with upturned brim. The Scarecrow wrapped himself in the purple robe, took off his old Munchkin hat, and substituted the Imperial headpiece.

"How do I look, Chew?" he asked anxiously.

"Quite like your old Imperial Self, except—" The old Prime Minister ran unsteadily out of the room. There was a muffled scream from the hall, and the next instant he returned with a long, shiny, silver queue which he had evidently clipped from the head of one of the servants. Removing the Scarecrow's hat, he pinned the queue to the back, set it on the Scarecrow's head, and stood regarding him with great satisfaction. "Ah, if the Empress could only see you!" he murmured rapturously.

"Where—where is she?" asked the Scarecrow, looking around nervously. His long, care-free life in Oz had somewhat unfitted him, he reflected, for family life.

"Alas!" sighed the Grand Chew Chew, wiping his eyes on the sleeve of his kimono, "She has returned to her silver ancestors."

"Then show me her picture," commanded the Scarecrow, visibly affected. The Grand Chew Chew stepped to a side wall, and pulling on a silken cord, disclosed the picture of a large, grey lady with curiously small eyes and a curiously large nose.

"Is she not beautiful?" asked the Grand Chew Chew, bowing his head. "Beautiful—er—er, beautiful!" gulped the Scarecrow. He thought of lovely little Ozma and dear little Dorothy, and all at once felt terribly upset and homesick. He had no recollection of the Silver Island or his life here whatever. Who was he, anyway—the Scarecrow of Oz or Emperor Chang Wang Woe? He couldn't be both.

"Ah!" whispered the Grand Chew Chew, seeing his agitation. "You remember her?" The Scarecrow shook his head, with an inward shudder.

"Now show me myself, Chew," he asked curiously. Pulling the cord of a portrait beside the Empress, Chew Chew revealed the picture of Chang Wang Woe as he had been fifty years ago. His face was bland and jolly, and to be perfectly truthful, quite like the Scarecrow's in shape and expression. "I am beside myself," murmured the Scarecrow dazedly— which in truth he was.

"You were—er—are a very royal and handsome person," stammered the Grand Chew Chew.

The Scarecrow, stepping off the throne to examine himself more closely, dropped the little fan and parasol. He had really not had time to examine them since they snapped off the beanstalk, and now, looking at them carefully, he found them extremely pretty.

"Dorothy will like these," thought the Scarecrow, slipping them into a large inside pocket of his robe. Already, in the back of his head, was a queer notion that he would at some time or other return to Oz. He started to give the Grand Chew Chew a spirited description of that wonderful country, but the ancient gentleman yawned and, waving his hands toward the door, interrupted him with:

"Would not your Supreme Highness care to inspect your present dominions?"

"I suppose I may as well!" With a deep sigh, the Scarecrow took the Grand Chew Chew's arm and, holding up his royal kimono (which was rather long) with the other hand, walked unsteadily down the great salon. They were about to pass into the garden when a little fat Silverman slid around the door, a huge silver drumstick upraised in his right hand and a great drum hung about his neck.

The drummer beamed on the Scarecrow.

"Chang Wang Woe, the Beautiful,

The Beautiful has come!
Sublime and silver Scarecrow,
Let sound the royal drum!"

chanted the little man in a high, thin voice, and started to bring the drumstick down upon the huge head of his noisy instrument.

"No you don't!" cried the Scarecrow, leaping forward and catching his arm.

"I positively forbid it!"

"Then I shall have no work!" screamed the drummer, falling on his face. "Ah, Gracious Master, don't you remember me?"

"Yes," said the Scarecrow kindly, "who are you?"

"Oh, don't you remember little Happy Toko?" wheezed the little man, the tears rolling down his cheeks. "I was only a boy, but you used to be fond of me."

"Why, of course, my dear Tappy," said the Scarecrow, not liking to hurt the little fellow's feelings. "But why do you beat the drum?"

"It is customary to sound the drum at the approach of your Royal Highness," put in the Grand Chew Chew importantly.

"Was customary," said the Scarecrow firmly. "My dear Tappy Oko, never sound it in my presence again; it is too upsetting." Which was true enough, for one blow of the drum sent the flimsy Scarecrow flying into the air.

"You're dismissed, Happy," snapped the Grand Chew Chew. At this, the little Silver Islander began weeping and roaring with distress.

"Stop! What else can you do besides beat a drum?" asked the Scarecrow kindly.

"I can sing, stand on my head, and tell jokes," sniffed Happy Toko, shuffling from one foot to the other.

"Very good," said the Scarecrow. "You are henceforth Imperial Punster to my Person. Come along, we're going to look over the Island."

The Grand Chew Chew frowned so terribly that Happy Toko's knees shook with terror.

"It is not fitting for a slave to accompany the Grand Chew Chew and the Emperor," he hissed angrily.

The Scarecrow looked surprised, for the Kingdom of Oz is quite democratic, and no one is considered better than another. But seeing this was not the time to argue, he winked broadly behind the

Grand Chew Chew's back.

"I'll see you again, Tappy my boy," he called genially, and passed out into the garden, where a magnificent silver palanquin, surrounded by pikemen and shieldbearers, awaited him.

Chapter 8

The Scarecrow Studies the Silver Island

Two days had passed since the Scarecrow had fallen into his Kingdom. He was not finding his royal duties as pleasant as he had anticipated. The country was beautiful enough, but being Emperor of the Silver Islands was not the simple affair that ruling Oz had been. The pigtail on the back of his hat was terribly distracting, and he was always tripping over his kimono, to which he could not seem to accustom himself. His subjects were extremely quarrelsome, always pulling one another's queues or stealing fruit, umbrellas, and silver polish. His ministers, the Grand Chew Chew, the Chief Chow Chow, and General Mugwump, were no better, and keeping peace in the palace took all the Scarecrow's cleverness.

In the daytime he tried culprits in the royal court, interviewed his seventeen secretaries, rode out in the royal palanquin, and made speeches to visiting princes. At night he sat in the great silver salon and by the light of the lanterns studied the Book of Ceremonies. His etiquette, the Grand Chew Chew informed him, was shocking. He was always doing something wrong, dodging the Imperial Umbrella, speaking kindly to a palace servant, or walking unattended in the gardens.

The royal palace itself was richly furnished, and the Scarecrow had more than five hundred robes of state. The gardens, with their sparkling waterfalls, glowing orange trees, silver temples, towers and bridges, were too lovely for words. Poppies, roses, lotus and other lilies perfumed the air, and at night a thousand silver lanterns turned them to a veritable fairyland.

The grass and trees were green as in other lands, but the sky as always full of tiny silver clouds, the waters surrounding the island were of a lovely liquid silver, and as all the houses and towers were of this gleaming metal, the effect was bewildering and beautiful.

But the Silver Islanders themselves were too stupid to appreciate this beauty. "And what use is it all when I have no one to enjoy it with me," sighed the Scarecrow. "And no time to *play*!"

In Oz no one thought it queer if Ozma, the little Queen, jumped rope with Dorothy or Betsy Bobbin, or had a quiet game of croquet with the palace cook. But here, alas, everything was different. If the Scarecrow so much as ventured a game of ball with the gardener's boy, the whole court was thrown into an uproar. At first, the Scarecrow tried to please everybody, but finding that nothing pleased the people in the palace, he decided to please himself.

"I don't care a kinkajou if I am the Emperor, I'm going to talk to whom I please!" he exclaimed on the second night, and shaking his glove at a bronze statue, he threw the Book of Ceremonies into the fountain. The next morning, therefore, he ascended the throne with great firmness. Immediately, the courtiers prostrated themselves, and the Scarecrow's arms and legs blew about wildly.

"Stand up at once," puffed the Scarecrow when he had regained his balance.

"You are giving me nervous prostration. Chew, kindly issue an edict forbidding prostrations. Anyone caught bowing in my presence again shall lose—" the courtiers looked alarmed "— his pigtail!" finished the Scarecrow.

"And now, Chew, you will take my place, please. I am going for a walk with Tappy Oko."

The Grand Chew Chew's mouth fell open with surprise, but seeing the Scarecrow's determined expression, he dared not disobey, and he immediately began making strange marks on a long, red parchment. Happy Toko trembled as the Scarecrow Emperor took his arm, and the courtiers stared at one another in dismay as the two walked quietly out into the garden.

Nothing happened, however, and Tappy, regaining his composure, took out a little silver flute and started a lively tune.

"I had to take matters into my own hands, Tappy," said the Scarecrow, listening to the music with a pleased expression. "Are there any words to that song?"

"Yes, illustrious and Supreme Sir!"

> *"Two spoons went down a Por-ce-Lane,*
> *To meet a China saucer,*
> *A 'talking China in a way*
> *To break a white man's jaw, Sir!"*

sang Happy, and finished by standing gravely on his

head.

"Your Majesty used to be very fond of this song," spluttered Happy. (It is difficult to speak while upside down, and if you don't think so, try it!)

"Ah!" said the Scarecrow, beginning to feel more cheerful, "Tell me something about myself and my family, Tappy Oko."

"Happy Toko, if it pleases your Supreme Amiability," corrected the little silver man, somersaulting to a standstill beside the Scarecrow.

"It does and it doesn't," murmured the Scarecrow. "There is something about you that reminds me of a pudding, and you tapped the drum, didn't you? I believe I shall call you Tappy Oko, if you don't mind!"

The Scarecrow seated himself on a silver bench and motioned for the Imperial Punster to sit down beside him. Tappy Oko sat down fearfully, first making sure that he was not observed.

"Saving your Imperial Presence, this is not permitted," said Tappy uneasily.

"Never mind about my Imperial Presence," chuckled the Scarecrow. "Tell me about my Imperial Past."

"Ah!" said Tappy Oko, rolling up his eyes, "You

were one of the most magnificent and magnanimous of monarchs."

"Was I?" asked the Scarecrow in a pleased voice.

"You distributed rice among the poor, and advice among the rich, and fought many glorious battles," continued the little man. ""I composed a little song about you. Perhaps you would like to hear it?"

The Scarecrow nodded, and Tappy, throwing back his head, chanted with a will:

> *"Chang Wang Woe did draw the bow-*
> *And twist the queues of a thousand foe!"*

"In Oz," murmured the Scarecrow reflectively as Tappy finished, "I twisted the necks of a flock of wild crows—that was before I had my excellent brains, too. Oh, I'm a fighting man, there's no doubt about it. But tell me, Tappy, where did I meet my wife?"

"In the water!" chuckled Tappy Oko, screwing up his eyes.

"Never!" The Scarecrow looked out over the harbour and then down at his lumpy figure.

"Your Majesty forgets you were then a man like me—er—not stuffed with straw, I mean," exclaimed Happy, looking embarrassed. "She was fishing," continued the little Punster, "when a huge silver fish became entangled in her line. She stood up, the fish gave a mighty leap and pulled her out of the boat. Your Majesty, having seen the whole affair from the bank, plunged bravely into the water and, swimming out, rescued her, freed the fish, and in due time made her your bride. I've made a song about that, also."

"Let's hear it," said the Scarecrow. And this is what Happy sung:

> *"Tsing Tsing, a Silver Fisher's daughter,*
> *Was fishing in the silver water.*
> *The moon shone on her silver hair*
> *And there were fishes everywhere!"*

> *"Then came a mighty silver fish,*
> *It seized her line and with a swish*
> *Of silver fins upset her boat.*
> *Tsing Tsing could neither swim nor float."*

> *"She raised her silver voice in fear*

And who her call of help should hear
But Chang Wang Woe, the Emperor,
Who saved and married her, what's more!"

"Did I really?" asked the Scarecrow, feeling quite flattered by Happy's song.

"Yes," said Happy positively, "and invited me to the wedding, though I was only a small boy."

"Was Chew Chew there?" The Scarecrow couldn't help wondering how the old Nobleman had taken his marriage with a poor fisherman's daughter.

Happy chuckled at the memory. "He had a Princess all picked out for you," he confided merrily:

"And there he stood in awful pride
And scorned the father of the bride!"

"Hoh!" roared the Scarecrow, falling off the bench. "That's the Ozziest thing I've heard since I landed in the Silver Islands. Tappy, my boy, I believe we are going to be friends! But let's forget the past and think of the present!"

The Scarecrow embraced his Imperial Punster on the spot. "Let's find something jolly to do," he suggested.

"Would your Extreme Highness care for kites?" asked Happy. "'Tis a favourite sport here!"

"Would I! But wait, I will disguise myself." Hiding his royal hat under the bench, he put on Happy Toko's broad-rimmed peasant hat. It turned down all 'round and almost hid his face. Then he turned his robe inside out and declared himself ready.

They passed through a small silver town before they reached the field where the kites were to be flown, and the Scarecrow was delighted with its picturesque and quaint appearance. The streets were narrow and full of queer shops. Silver lanterns and little pennants hung from each door, the merchants and maidens in their gay sedans and the people afoot made a bright and lively picture.

"If I could just live here instead of in the palace," mused the Scarecrow, pausing before a modest rice shop. It is dangerous to stop in the narrow streets, and Happy jerked his master aside just in time to prevent his being trodden on by a huge camel. It sniffed at the Scarecrow suspiciously, and they were forced to flatten themselves against a wall to let it pass. Happy anxiously hurried the Emperor through the town, and they soon arrived at the kite flying field. A great throng had gathered to watch the exhibition, and there were more kites than one would see in a lifetime here. Huge fish, silver paper dragons, birds—every sort and shape of kite was tugging at its string, and hundreds of Silver Islanders—boys, girls and grown-ups—were looking on.

"How interesting," said the Scarecrow, fascinated by a huge dragon that floated just over his head. "I wish Dorothy could see this, I do indeed!"

But the dragon kite seemed almost alive, and horrors! Just as it swooped down, a hook in the tail caught in the Scarecrow's collar, and before Happy Toko could even wink, the Emperor of the Silver Islands was sailing towards the clouds. The Scarecrow, as you must know, weighs almost nothing, and the people shouted with glee, for they thought him a dummy man and part of the performance. But Happy Toko ran after the kite as fast as his fat little legs would carry him.

"Alas, alas, I shall lose my position!" wailed Happy Toko, quite convinced that the Scarecrow would be dashed to pieces on the rocks. "Oh, putty head that I am to set myself against the Grand Chew Chew!"

The Scarecrow, however, after recovering from the first shock, began to enjoy himself. Holding fast to the dragon's tail, he looked down with great interest upon his dominions. Rocks, mountains, tall silver pagodas, drooping willow trees, flashed beneath him. Truly a beautiful island! His gaze strayed over the silver waters surrounding the island, and he was astonished to see a great fleet sailing into the harbour—a great fleet of singular vessels with silken sails.

"What's this?" thought the Scarecrow. But just then the dragon kite became suddenly possessed. It jerked him up, it jerked him down, and shook him this way and that. His hat flew off, his arms and legs whirled wildly, and pieces of straw began to float downward. Then the hook ripped and tore through his coat and, making a terrible slit in his back, came out. Down, down, down flashed the Scarecrow and landed in a heap on the rocks. Poor Happy Toko rushed toward him with streaming eyes.

"Oh radiant and immortal Scarecrowcus, what have they done to you?" he moaned, dropping on his knees beside the flimsy shape of the Emperor.

"Merely knocked out my honourable stuffing," mumbled the Scarecrow. "Now Tappy, my dear fellow, will you just turn me over? There's a rock in my eye that keeps me from thinking."

Happy Toko, at the sound of a voice from the rumpled heap of clothing, gave a great leap.

"Is there any straw about?" asked the Scarecrow anxiously. "Why don't you turn me over?"

"It's his ghost," moaned Happy Toko, and because he dared not disobey a royal ghost, he turned the Scarecrow over with trembling hands.

"Don't be alarmed," said the Scarecrow, smiling reassuringly. "I'm not breakable like you meat people. A little straw will make me good as new. A little straw—straw, do you hear?" For Happy's pigtail was still on end, and he was shaking so that his silver shoes clattered on the rocks.

"I command you to fetch straw!" cried the Scarecrow at last, in an angry voice. Happy dashed away.

When he returned with an arm full of straw, the Scarecrow managed to convince him that he was quite alive. "It is impossible to kill a person from Oz," he explained proudly, "and that is why my present figure is so much more satisfactory than yours. I do not have to eat or sleep and can always be repaired. Have you some safety pins?" Happy produced several and under the Scarecrow's direction stuffed out his chest and pinned up his rents.

"Let us return," said the Scarecrow. "I've had enough pleasure for one day, and can't you sing something, Tappy?" Running and fright had somewhat affected Happy's voice, but he squeaked out a funny little song, and the two, keeping time to the tune, came without further mishap to the Imperial gardens. Happy had just set the royal hat upon the Scarecrow's head and brushed off his robes when a company of courtiers dashed out of the palace door and came running toward them.

"Great Cornstarch!" exclaimed the Scarecrow, sitting heavily down on the silver bench. "What's the matter now? Here are all the Pig-heads on the Island, and look how old Chew Chew is puffing!"

"One would expect a Chew Chew to puff," observed Happy slyly. "One would—" But he got no further, for the whole company was upon them.

"Save us! Save us!" wailed the courtiers, forgetting the royal edict and falling on their faces.

"What from?" asked the Scarecrow, holding fast to the silver bench.

"The King—the King of the Golden Islands!" shrieked the Grand Chew Chew.

"Ah yes!" murmured the Scarecrow, frowning thoughtfully. "Was that his fleet coming into the harbour?"

The Grand Chew Chew jumped up in astonishment. "How could your Highness see the fleet from here?" he stuttered.

"Not from here—there," said the Scarecrow, pointing upward and winking at Happy Toko. "My Highness goes very high, you see!"

"Your Majesty does not seem to realize the seriousness of the matter," choked the Grand Chew Chew. "He will set fire to the island and make us all slaves." At this, the courtiers began banging their heads distractedly on the grass.

"Set fire to the island!" exclaimed the Scarecrow, jumping to his feet. "Then peace to my ashes! Tappy, will you see that they are sent back to Oz?"

"Save us! Save us!" screamed the frightened Silvermen.

"The prophecy of the beanstalk has promised that you would save us. You are the Emperor Chang Wang Woe," persisted the Grand Chew Chew, waving his long arms.

"Woe is me," murmured the Scarecrow, clasping his yellow gloves. "But let me think."

Chapter 9

"Save Us with Your Magic, Exalted One!"

For several minutes, the Scarecrow sat perfectly still while the company stood shaking in their shoes. Then he asked loudly, "Where is the Imperial Army?"

"It has retired to the caves at the end of the Island," quavered the Grand Chew Chew.

"I thought as much," said the Scarecrow. "But never mind, there are quite a lot of us."

"Us!" spluttered a tall Silverman indignantly. "We are not common soldiers."

"No, very uncommon ones, but you have hard heads and long nails, and I dare say will manage somehow. Come on, let's go. Chew, you may take the lead."

"Go!" shrieked the Grand Chew Chew. "Us?" The Courtiers began backing away in alarm. "Where—er—what—are your Highness' plans?"

"Why, just to conquer the King of the Golden Islands and send him back home," said the Scarecrow, smiling engagingly. "That's what you wanted, isn't it?"

"But it is not honourable for noblemen to fight. It—"

"Oh, of course, if you prefer burning—" The Scarecrow rose unsteadily and started for the garden gates. Not a person stirred. The Scarecrow looked back, and his reproachful face was too much for Happy Toko.

"I'll come, exalted and radiant Scarecrowcus! Wait, honourable and valiant Sir!"

"Bring a watering can, if you love me," called the Scarecrow over his shoulder, and Happy, snatching one from a frightened gardener, dashed after his Master.

"If things get too hot, I'd like to know that you can put me out," said the Scarecrow, his voice quivering with emotion. "You shall be rewarded for this, my brave Tappy."

Happy did not answer, for his teeth were chattering so he could not speak.

The harbour lay just below the Imperial Palace, and the Scarecrow and Happy hurried on through the crowds of fleeing Silvermen, their household goods packed upon their heads. Some cheered faintly for Chang Wang Woe, but none offered to follow, save the faithful Happy.

"Is this king old?" asked the Scarecrow, looking anxiously at the small boats full of warriors that were putting out from the fleet.

"He is the son of the King whom your Majesty conquered fifty years ago," gulped Happy. "Ha—has your Imperial Highness any—plan?"

"Not yet," said the Scarecrow cheerfully, "but I'm thinking very hard."

"Then, goodbye to Silver Island!" choked Happy Toko, dropping the watering can with a crash.

"Never mind," said the Scarecrow kindly. "If they shoot me and I catch fire, I'll jump in the water and you must fish me out, Tappy. Now please don't talk any more. I must think!"

Poor Happy Toko had nothing else to say, for he considered his day finished. The first of the invaders were already landing on the beach, and standing up in a small boat, encased in glittering gold armour, was the King of the Golden Islands, himself. The sun was quite hot, and there was a smell of gunpowder in the air.

Now the Scarecrow had encountered many dangers in Oz and had usually thought his way out of them, but as they came nearer and nearer to the shore and no idea presented itself, he began to feel extremely nervous. A bullet fired from the king's boat tore through his hat, and the smoke made him more anxious than ever about his straw stuffing. He felt hurriedly in his pocket, and his clumsy fingers closed over the little fan he had plucked from the bean pole.

Partly from agitation and partly because he did not know what else to do, the Scarecrow flipped the fan open. At that minute, a mighty roar went up from the enemy, for at the first motion of the fan they had been jerked fifty feet into the air, and there they hung suspended over their ships, kicking and squealing for dear life. The Scarecrow was as surprised as they, and as for Happy Toko, he fell straightway on his nose!

"Magic!" exclaimed the Scarecrow. "Someone is helping us," and he began fanning himself gently with the little fan, waiting to see what would happen next. At each wave of the fan, the King of the Golden Islands and his men flew higher until at last not one of them could be seen from the shore.

"The fan. The magic is in the fan!" gasped Happy Toko, jumping up and embracing the Scarecrow.

"Why, what do you mean?" asked the Scarecrow, closing the fan with a snap. Happy's answer was drowned in a huge splash. As soon as the fan was closed, down whirled the king's army into the sea, and each man struck the water with such force that the spray rose high as a skyscraper. And not till then did the Scarecrow realize the power of the little fan he had been saving for Dorothy.

"Saved!" screamed Happy Toko, dancing up and down. "Hurrah for the Emperor!"

"The Emperor, without a plan,
Has won the victory with a fan."

The Silver Islanders had paused in their flight at the queer noises coming from the harbour, and now all of them, hearing Tappy Oko's cries, came crowding down to the shore and were soon cheering themselves hoarse. No wonder! The drenched soldiers of the king were climbing swiftly back into their boats, and when they were all aboard, the Scarecrow waved his fan sidewise (he did not want to blow them up again), and the ships swept out of the harbour so fast that the water churned to silver suds behind them, and they soon were out of sight.

"Ah!" cried the Grand Chew Chew, arriving breathlessly at this point, "We have won the day!"

"So we have!" chuckled the Scarecrow, putting his arm around Happy Toko. "Call the brave army and decorate the generals!"

"It shall be done," said the Grand Chew Chew, frowning at Happy. "There shall be a great celebration, a feast, and fireworks."

"Fireworks," quavered the Scarecrow, clutching his Imperial Punster. By this time, the Silver Islanders were crowding around the Emperor, shouting and squealing for joy, and before he could prevent it, they had placed him on their shoulders and carried him in triumph to the palace. He managed to signal Happy, and Happy nodded reassuringly and ran off as fast as his fat little legs could patter. He arrived at the palace almost as soon as the Scarecrow, lugging a giant silver watering can, and, sitting calmly on the steps of the throne, fanned himself with his hat. The Scarecrow eyed the watering can with satisfaction.

"Now let them have their old fireworks,"

he muttered under his breath, and settled himself comfortably. The Grand Chew Chew was hopping about like a ditched kite, arranging for the celebration. The courtiers were shaking hands with themselves and forming in a long line. A great table was being set in the hall.

"What a fuss they are making over nothing," said the Scarecrow to Happy Toko. "Now in Oz when we win a victory, we all play some jolly game and sit down to dinner with Ozma. Why, they haven't even set a place for you, Happy!"

"I'd rather sit here, amiable Master," sighed Happy Toko happily. "Is the little fan safely closed?"

The Scarecrow felt in his pocket to make sure, then leaned forward in surprise. The Royal Silver Army were marching stiffly into the hall, and the courtiers were bobbing and bowing and cheering like mad.

The General came straight to the great silver throne, clicked his silver heels, bowed, and stood at attention.

"Well," said the Scarecrow, surveying this splendid person curiously, "what is it?"

"They have come for their decorations," announced the Grand Chew Chew, stepping up with a large silver platter full of medals.

"But I thought Tappy Oko and I saved the Island," chuckled the Scarecrow, nudging the Imperial Punster.

"Had the Imperial Army not retired and left the field to you, there would have been no victory," faltered the General in a timid voice. "Therefore, in a way we are responsible for the victory. A great general always knows when to retire."

"There's something in that," admitted the Scarecrow, scratching his head thoughtfully. "Go ahead and decorate 'em, Chew Chew!"

This the Grand Chew Chew proceeded to do, making such a long speech to each soldier that half of the Court fell asleep and the Scarecrow fidgeted uncomfortably.

"They remind me of the Army of Oz," he confided to Happy Toko, "but we never have long speeches in Oz. I declare, I wish I could go to sleep, too, and that's something I have never seen any use in before."

"They've just begun," yawned Happy Toko, nearly rolling down the steps of the throne, and Happy was not far wrong, for all afternoon one after the other of the courtiers arose and droned about the great victory, and as they all addressed themselves to the Scarecrow, he was forced to listen politely. When the speeches were over, there was still the grand banquet to be got through, and as the Silver Islanders ate much the same fare as their Chinese cousins, you can imagine the poor Scarecrow's feelings.

"Ugh!" shivered the Scarecrow as the strange dishes appeared, "I'm glad none of my friends are here. How fortunate that I'm stuffed with straw!" The broiled mice, the stewed shark fins and the bird nest soup made him stare. He had ordered Happy Toko to be placed at his side, and to watch him happily at work with his silver chopsticks and porcelain spoon was the only satisfaction he got out of the feast.

"And what is that?" he asked, pointing to a steaming bowl that had just been placed before Happy.

"Minced cat, your Highness," replied Happy, sprinkling it generously with silver polish.

"Cat?" shrieked the Scarecrow, pouncing to his feet in horror. "Do you mean to tell me you are eating a poor, innocent, little cat?"

"Not a poor one at all. A very rich one, I should say," replied Happy Toko with his mouth full. "Ah, had your Highness only your old body, how you would enjoy this!"

"Never!" shouted the Scarecrow so loudly that all of the Courtiers looked up in surprise. "How dare you eat innocent cats?" Indignantly he thought of Dorothy's pet kitten back in Oz. Oz—why had he ever left that wonderful country?

"Your Highness has eaten hundreds," announced the Grand Chew Chew calmly. "Hundreds!"

The Scarecrow dropped back into his chair, too shocked for speech. He, the Scarecrow of Oz, had eaten hundreds of cats! What would Dorothy say to that? Ugh! This was his first experience with Silver Island fare. He had always spent the dinner hours in the garden. He sighed, and looked wistfully at the bean pole in the centre of the hall. Every minute he was feeling less and less like the Emperor of the Silver Island and more and more like the plain Scarecrow of Oz.

"Your Majesty seems out of spirits," said Happy Toko as he placed himself and the huge watering can beside the Emperor's bench in the garden later in the evening.

"I wish I were," said the Scarecrow. "To have an Emperor's spirit wished on you is no joke, my dear Tappy. It's a blinking bore!" At that moment, the fireworks commenced. The garden, ablaze with many shaped silver lanterns, looked more like Fairyland than ever. But each rocket made the Scarecrow wince. Showers of stars and butterflies fell 'round his head, fiery dragons leaped over the trees, and in all the Fourth of July celebrations you could imagine there were never such marvellous fireworks as these. No wonder Happy Toko, gazing in delight, forgot his promises to his Royal Master.

Soon the Scarecrow's fears were realized, and his straw stuffing began to smoke.

"Put me out! Put me out!" cried the Scarecrow, as a shower of sparks settled in his lap. The royal band made such a din and the courtiers such a clatter that Happy did not hear.

All of the Silver Islanders were intent on the display, and they forgot all about their unhappy and smoking Emperor.

"Help! Water! Water! Fire!" screamed the Scarecrow, jumping off his throne and knocking Happy head over heels. Thus brought to his senses, Happy hurriedly seized the watering can and sprinkled its contents on the smoking Emperor.

"Am I out?" gasped the Emperor anxiously.

"A fine way to celebrate a victory, lighting me up like a Roman candle!"

"Yes, dear Master," said the repentant Happy, helping the dripping Scarecrow to his feet, "it only scorched your royal robe. And it's all over, anyway. Let us go in."

The dripping Emperor was quite ready to follow his Imperial Punster's advice.

"Now that I am put out, let us by all means go in," said the Scarecrow gloomily, and the two slipped off without anyone noticing their departure.

"I'm afraid I'll have to have some new stuffing tomorrow," observed the Scarecrow, sinking dejectedly on his throne. "Tappy, my dear boy, after this never leave me alone, do you hear?" Happy Toko made no reply. He had fallen asleep beside the Imperial Throne.

The Scarecrow might have called his court, but he was in no mood for more of the Silver Islanders' idea of a good time. He longed for the dear friends of his loved Land of Oz.

One by one the lights winked out in the gardens, and the noisy company dispersed, and soon no one in the palace was awake but the Scarecrow. His straw was wet and soggy, and even his excellent brains felt damp and dull.

"If it weren't for Tappy Oko, how lonely I should be." He stared through the long, dim, empty hall with its shimmering silver screens and vases. "I wonder what little Dorothy is doing," sighed the Scarecrow wistfully.

Chapter 10

Princess Ozma and Betsy Bobbin Talk it Over

"Dorothy must be having a lovely time at the Scarecrow's," remarked Betsy Bobbin to Ozma one afternoon as they sat reading in the Royal Gardens several days after Dorothy's departure from the Emerald City of Oz.

"One always has a jolly time at the Scarecrow's," laughed the little Queen of Oz. "I must look in my Magic Picture and see what they are doing.

Too bad she missed the A-B-Sea Serpent and Rattlesnakes. Weren't they the funniest creatures?"

Both the little girls (for Ozma is really just a little girl) went off into a gale of laughter. The two queer creatures had followed the Scarecrow's advice and had spent their vacation in the Emerald City, and partly because they were so dazzled by their surroundings and partly because they have no sort of memories whatever, they never mentioned the Scarecrow himself or said anything about his plan to hunt his family tree. They talked incessantly of the Mer City and told innumerable A-B-Sea stories to Scraps and the Tin Woodman and the children of the Emerald City. When they were ready to go, the A-B-Sea Serpent snapped off its X block for Ozma. X, he said, meant almost everything, and pretty well expressed his gratitude to the lovely little ruler of Oz. Ozma in turn gave each of the visitors an emerald collar, and that very morning they had started back to the Munchkin River, and all the celebrities of Oz had gotten up to see them off.

"Maybe they'll come again sometime," said Betsy Bobbin, swinging her feet. "But look, Ozma, here comes a messenger." A messenger it surely was, dressed in the quaint red costume of the Quadlings. It was from Glinda, the Good Sorceress, and caused the Princess to sigh with vexation.

"Tell Jack Pumpkinhead to harness the Sawhorse to the red wagon," said Ozma after glancing hastily at the little note. "The Horners and Hoppers are at war again. And tell the Wizard to make ready for a journey."

"May I come, too?" asked Betsy. Ozma nodded with a troubled little frown, and Betsy bustled off importantly. Not many little girls are called upon to help settle wars and rule a country as wonderful as Oz.

The Horners and Hoppers are a quarrelsome and curious folk living in the Quadling Mountains, and soon Ozma, Jack Pumpkinhead, Betsy and the Wizard of Oz were rattling off at the best speed the Sawhorse could manage. This was pretty fast, for the little horse, being made of wood and magically brought to life, never tires and could outrun anything on legs in the fairy Kingdom of Oz.

But the fact that interests us is that Ozma did not look in the Magic Picture or see what exciting adventures the Scarecrow and Dorothy really were having!

As for Professor Wogglebug, who had caused all the trouble, he was busily at work on the twelfth chapter of the Royal Book of Oz, which he had modestly headed:

H. M. WOGGLEBUG T.E., PRINCE OF BUGS,

Cultured and Eminent Educator
and also
Great Grand and General Genealogist of Oz.

Chapter 11

Sir Hokus Overcometh the Giant

"I don't believe we'll ever find the way out of this forest."

Dorothy stopped with a discouraged little sigh and leaned against a tree. They had followed the road for several hours. First it had been fine and wide, but it had gradually dwindled to a crooked little path that wound crazily in and out through the trees. Although it was almost noonday, not a ray of sun penetrated through the dim green depths.

"Methinks," said Sir Hokus, peering into the gloom ahead, "that a great adventure is at hand."

The Cowardly Lion put back his ears. "What makes you methink so?" he rumbled anxiously.

"Hark thee!" said Sir Hokus, holding up his finger warningly. From a great way off sounded a curious thumping. It was coming nearer and nearer.

"Good gracious!" cried Dorothy, catching hold of the Cowardly Lion's mane.

"This is worse than Pokes!"

"Perchance it is a dragon," exulted the Knight, drawing his short sword. "Ah, how it would refresh me to slay a dragon!"

"I don't relish dragons myself. Scorched my tongue on one once," said the Cowardly Lion huskily. "But I'll fight with you, brother Hokus. Stand back, Dorothy dear."

As the thuds grew louder, the Knight fairly danced up and down with excitement. "Approach, villain!" he roared lustily.

"Approach till I impale thee on my lance. Ah, had I but a horse!"

"I'd let you ride on my back if it weren't for that hard tin suit," said the Cowardly Lion. "But cheer up, my dear Hokus, your voice is a little hoarse." Dorothy giggled nervously, then seized hold of a small tree, for the whole forest was rocking.

"How now!" gasped the Knight. There was a terrific quake that threw Sir Hokus on his face and sent every hair in the lion's mane on end, and then a great foot came crashing down through the treetops not three paces from the little party. Before they could even swallow, a giant hand flashed down-ward, jerked up a handful of trees by the roots, and disappeared, while a voice from somewhere way above shouted:

> *"What are little humans for?*
> *To feed the giant Bangladore.*
> *Broiled or toasted, baked or roasted,*
> *I smell three or maybe four!"*

"You hear that?" quavered the Cowardly Lion. Sir Hokus did not answer. His helmet had been jammed down by his fall, and he was tugging it upward with both hands. Frightened though Dorothy was, she ran to the Knight's assistance.

"Have at you!" cried Sir Hokus as soon as the opening in his helmet was opposite his eyes. "Forward!"

"My heart is beating a retreat," gulped the Cowardly Lion, but he bounded boldly after Sir Hokus.

"Varlet!" hissed the Knight, and raising his sword gave a mighty slash at the giant's ankle, which was broad as three tree trunks, while the Cowardly Lion gave a great spring and sank his teeth in the giant's huge leg.

"Ouch!" roared the giant in a voice that shook every leaf in the forest. "You stop, or I'll tell my father!" With that, he gave a hop that sent Sir Hokus flying into the treetops, stumbled over a huge rock, and came crashing to the earth, smashing trees like grass blades. At the giant's first scream, Dorothy shut her eyes and, putting her hands over her ears, had run as far and as fast as she could. At the awful crash, she stopped short, opened her eyes, and stared 'round giddily.

The giant was flat on his back, but as he was stretched as far as four city blocks, only half of him was visible. The Cowardly Lion still clung to his leg, and he was gurgling and struggling in a way Dorothy could not understand.

She looked around in a panic for the Knight. Just then, Sir Hokus dropped from the branch of a tree.

"Uds daggers!" he puffed, looking ruefully at his sword, which had snapped off at the handle, "'Tis a pretty rogue!"

"Don't you think we'd better run?" shiver Dorothy, thinking of the giant's song.

"Not while I wear these colours!" exclaimed

Sir Hokus, proudly touching Dorothy's hair ribbon, which still adorned his arm. "Come, my good Lion, let us dispatch this braggart and saucy monster."

"Father!" screamed the giant, making no attempt to move.

"He seems to be frightened, himself," whispered Dorothy to the Knight. "But whatever is the matter with the Cowardly Lion?"

At that minute, the Cowardly Lion gave a great jerk and began backing with his four feet braced. The piece of giant leg that he had hold of stretched and stretched, and while Sir Hokus and Dorothy stared in amazement, it snapped off and the Cowardly Lion rolled head over paws.

"Toffee!" roared the Cowardly Lion, sitting up and trying to open his jaws, which were firmly stuck together.

"Toffee!" At this, Sir Hokus sprang nimbly on the giant's leg, ran up his chest, and perched bravely on his peppermint collar.

"Surrender, Knave!" he demanded threateningly. Dorothy, seeing she could do nothing to help the Cowardly Lion, followed. On her way up, she broke off a tiny piece of his coat and found it most delicious chocolate.

"Why, he's all made of sweets!" she cried excitedly.

"Oh, hush!" sobbed the giant, rolling his great sourball eyes. "I'd be eaten in a minute if it were known."

"You were mighty anxious to eat us a while ago," said Dorothy, looking longingly at the giant's coat buttons. They seemed to be large marshmallows.

"Go away!" screamed the giant, shaking so that Dorothy slid into his vest pocket. "No one under forty feet is allowed in this forest!"

Dorothy climbed crossly out of the giant's pocket. "We didn't come because we wanted to," she assured him, wiping the chocolate off her nose.

"Odds bodikins! I cannot fight a great baby like this," sighed Sir Hokus, dodging just in time a great, sugary tear that had rolled down the giant's nose. "He's got to apologize for that song, though."

"Wait!" cried Dorothy suddenly. "I have an idea. If you set us down on the edge of the forest and give us all your vest buttons for lunch, we won't tell anyone you're made of candy. We'll let you go," she called loudly, for the giant had begun to sob again.

"Won't you? Will you?" sniffed the foolish giant.

"Never sing that song again!" commanded the Knight sternly.

"No, Sir," answered the giant meekly. "Did your dog chew much of my leg, Sir?" Then, before Dorothy or Sir Hokus had time to say a word, they were snatched up in sticky fingers and next minute were dropped with a thump in a large field of daisies.

"Oh!" spluttered Dorothy as the giant made off on his taffy legs. "Oh, we've forgotten the Cowardly Lion!" But at that minute, the giant reappeared, and the lion was dropped beside them.

"What's this? What's this?" growled the Cowardly Lion, looking around wildly.

"We got him to lift us out of the forest," explained Dorothy. "Have you swallowed the toffee?" The lion was still dizzy from his ride and only shook his head feebly.

Sir Hokus sighed and sat heavily down on a large rock. "There is no sort of honour, methinks, in overcoming a candy giant," he observed, looking wistfully at the plume still pinned to Dorothy's dress. "Ah, had it but been a proper fight!"

"You didn't know he was candy. I think you were just splendid." Jumping up, Dorothy fastened the plume in the Knight's helmet. "And you're talking just beautifully, more like a Knight every minute," she added with conviction. Sir Hokus tried not to look pleased.

"Give me a meat enemy! My teeth ache yet! First singing, then toffee-leg pulling! Gr-ugh! What next?" growled the Cowardly Lion.

"Why, lunch, if you feel like eating," said Dorothy, beginning to give out the vest buttons which the giant had obediently ripped off and left for them. They *were* marshmallows, the size of pie plates, and Dorothy and Sir Hokus found them quite delicious. The Cowardly Lion, however, after a doubtful sniff and sneeze from the powdered sugar, declined and went off to find something more to his taste.

"We had better take some of these along," said Dorothy when she and Sir Hokus had eaten several. "We may need them later."

"Everything is yellow, so we must be in the Winkie Country," announced the Cowardly Lion, who had just returned from his lunch. "There's a road, too."

"Mayhap it will take us to the jewelled city of your gracious Queen." Sir Hokus shaded his eyes and stared curiously at the long lane stretching invitingly ahead of them.

"Well, anyway, we're out of the forest and Pokes, and maybe we'll meet someone who will tell us about the Scarecrow. Come on!" cried Dorothy gaily. "I think we're on the right track this time."

Chapter 12

Dorothy and Sir Hokus Come to Fix City

The afternoon went pleasantly for the three travellers. The road was wide and shady and really seemed a bit familiar. Dorothy rode comfortably on the Cowardly Lion's back and to pass the time told Sir Hokus all about Oz. He was particularly interested in the Scarecrow.

"Grammercy! He should be knighted!" he exclaimed, slapping his knee, as Dorothy told how the clever straw man had helped outwit the Gnome King when that wicked little rascal had tried to keep them prisoners in his underground kingdom.

"But, go to! Where is the gallant man now?" The Knight sobered quickly. "Mayhap in need of a strong arm! Mayhap at the mercy of some terrible monster!"

"Oh, I hope not!" cried Dorothy, dismayed at so dark a picture. "Why, oh why, did he bother about his family tree?"

"Trust the Scarecrow to take care of himself," said the Cowardly Lion in a gruff voice. Nevertheless, he quickened his steps. "The sooner we reach the Emerald City, the sooner we'll know where he is!"

The country through which they were passing was beautiful, but quite deserted. About five o'clock, they came to a clear little stream, and after Dorothy and Sir Hokus had washed their faces and the Cowardly Lion had taken a little plunge, they all felt refreshed. Later they came to a fine pear orchard, and as no one was about they helped themselves generously.

The more Dorothy and the Cowardly Lion saw of Sir Hokus, the fonder of him they grew. He was so kind-hearted and so polite.

"He'll be great company for us back in the Emerald City," whispered the Cowardly Lion as the Knight went off to get Dorothy a drink from a little spring. "That is, if he forgets this grammercy, bludgeon stuff."

"I think it sounds lovely," said Dorothy, "and he's remembering more of it all the time. But I wonder why there are no people here. I do hope we meet some before night." But no person did they meet. As it grew darker, Sir Hokus' armour began to creak in a quite frightful manner. Armour is not meant for walking, and the poor Knight was stiff and tired, but he made no complaint.

"Need oiling, don't you?" asked the Cowardly Lion, peering anxiously at him through the gloom.

"Joints in my armour a bit rusty," puffed Sir Hokus, easing one foot and then the other. "Ah, had I my good horse!" He expressively waved a piece of the giant's button at which he had been nibbling.

"Better climb up behind Dorothy," advised the Cowardly Lion, but Sir Hokus shook his head, for he knew the lion was tired, too.

"I'll manage famously. This very night I may find me a steed!"

"How?" asked the lion with a yawn.

"If I sleep beneath these trees, I may have a Knight mare," chuckled Sir Hokus triumphantly.

"Br-rrr!" roared the Cowardly Lion while Dorothy clapped her hands. But they were not to sleep beneath the trees after all, for a sudden turn in the road brought them right to the gates of another city. They knew it must be a city because a huge, lighted sign hung over the gate.

"Fix City," read Dorothy. "What a funny

name!"

"Maybe they can fix us up," rumbled the lion, winking at Sir Hokus.

"Perchance we shall hear news of the valiant Scarecrow!" cried the Knight, and limping forward he thumped on the gate with his mailed fist. Dorothy and the Cowardly Lion pressed close behind him and waited impatiently for someone to open the gate.

A bell rang loud back in the town. The next instant, the gates flew open so suddenly that the three adventurers were flung violently on their faces.

"Out upon them!" blustered Sir Hokus, getting up stiffly and running to help Dorothy. "What way is this to welcome strangers?" He pulled the little girl hastily to her feet, then they all ran forward, for the gates were swinging shut again.

It was almost as light as day, for lanterns were everywhere, but strangely enough they seemed to dart about like huge fireflies, and Dorothy ducked involuntarily as a red one bobbed down almost in her face. Then she gasped in real earnest and caught hold of Sir Hokus.

"Uds daggers!" wheezed the Knight. Two large bushes were running down the path, and right in front of Dorothy the larger caught the smaller and began pulling out its leaves.

"Leave off! Leave off!" screamed the little bush.

"That's what I'm doing," said the big bush savagely. "There won't be a leaf on when I get through with you."

"Unhand him, villain!" cried Sir Hokus, waving his sword at the large bush. The two bushes looked up in surprise, and when they saw Dorothy, the Cowardly Lion and Sir Hokus, they fell into each other's branches and burst into the most uproarious laughter.

"My dear Magnolia, this is rich! Oh, dear fellow, wait till Sit sees this; he will be convulsed!" Quite forgetting their furious quarrel, the two went rollicking down the path together, stopping every few minutes to look back and laugh at the three strangers.

"Is this usual?" asked Sir Hokus, looking quite dazed.

"I never heard of bushes talking or running around, but I confess I'm a few centuries behind times!"

"Neither did I!" exclaimed Dorothy. "But then—almost anything's likely to happen in Oz."

"If these lanterns don't look out something will happen. I'll break 'em to bits," growled the Cowardly Lion, who had been dodging half a dozen at once.

"How would we look—out?" sniffed one, flying at Dorothy.

"You could light out—or go out," giggled the little girl.

"We never go out unless we're put out," cried another, but as the Cowardly Lion made a few springs, they flew high into the air and began talking indignantly among themselves. By this time, the three had become accustomed to the changing lights.

"I wonder where the people are," said Dorothy, peering down a wide avenue. "There don't seem to be any houses. Oh, look!"

Three tables set for dinner with the most appetizing viands were walking jauntily down the street, talking fluent china.

"There must be people!" cried Dorothy.

"One dinner for each of us," rumbled the Cowardly Lion, licking his chops. "Come on!"

"Perchance they will invite us. If we follow the dinners, we'll come to the diners," said Sir Hokus mildly.

"Right—as usual." The Cowardly Lion looked embarrassed, for he had intended pouncing on the tables without further ceremony.

"Hush! Let's go quietly. If they hear us, they may run and upset the dishes," warned Dorothy. So the three walked softly after the dinner tables, their curiosity about the people of Fix growing keener at every step. Several chairs, a sofa and a clothes tree rushed past them, but as Dorothy said later to Ozma, after talking bushes, nothing surprised them. The tables turned the corner at the end of the avenue three abreast, and the sight that greeted Dorothy and her comrades was strange indeed. Down each side of a long street as far as they could see stood rows and rows of people. Each one was in the exact centre of a chalked circle, and they were so still that Dorothy thought they must be statues.

But no sooner had the three tables made their appearance than bells began ringing furiously all up and down the street, and dinner tables and chairs came running from every direction. All the inhabitants of Fix City looked alike. They had large, round heads, broad placid faces, double chins, and no waists whatever. Their feet were flat and about three times as long as the longest you have ever seen. The women wore plain Mother Hubbard dresses and straw sailor hats, and the men gingham suits.

While the three friends were observing all this, the tables had been taking their places. One stopped before each Fix, and the chairs, after much bumping and quarrelling, placed themselves properly. At a signal from the Fix in the centre, the whole company sat down without so much as moving their feet. Dorothy, Sir Hokus and the Cowardly Lion had been too interested to speak, but at this minute a whole flock of the mischievous lanterns clustered over their heads, and at the sudden blare of light the whole street stopped eating and stared.

"Oh!" cried the Fix nearest them, pointing with his fork, "Look at the runabouts!"

"This way, please! This way, please! Don't bark your shins. Don't take any more steps than you can help!" boomed an important voice from the middle of the street. So down the centre marched the three, feeling—as the Cowardly Lion put it—exactly like a circus.

"Stop! Names, please!" The Fix next to the centre put up his knife commandingly. Sir Hokus stepped forward with a bow:

"Princess Dorothy of Oz, the Cowardly Lion of Oz."

"And Sir Hokus of Pokes," roared the Lion as the Knight modestly stepped back without announcing himself.

"Sir Pokus of Hoax, Howardly Kion of Boz, and Little Girl Beginning with D," bellowed the Fix, "meet His Royal Highness, King Fix It, and the noble Fixitives."

"Little Girl Beginning with D! That's too long," complained the King, who, with the exception of his crown, looked like all the rest of them, "I'll leave out the middle. What do you want, Little With D?"

"My name is Dorothy, and if your Highness could give us some dinner and tell us something about the Scarecrow and—"

"One thing at a time, please," said the King reprovingly. "What does Poker want, and Boz? Have they anything to spend?"

"Only the night, an' it please your Gracious Highness," said Sir Hokus with his best bow.

"It doesn't please me especially," said the King, taking a sip of water. "And there! You've brought up another question. How do you want to spend it?"

He folded his hands helplessly on the table and looked appealingly at the Fix next to him. "How am I to settle all these questions, Sticken? First they come running around like crazy chairs, and—"

"You might ring for a settle," suggested Sticken, looking curiously at Sir Hokus. The King leaned back with a sigh of relief, then touched a bell. There were at least twenty bells set on a high post at his right hand, and all of the Fixes seemed to have similar bell posts.

"He's talking perfect nonsense," said Dorothy angrily. The Cowardly Lion began to roll his eyes ominously.

"Let me handle this, my dear. I'm used to Kings," whispered Sir Hokus. "Most of 'em talk nonsense. But if he grows wroth, we'll have all the furniture in the place around our ears. Now just—"

Bump! Sir Hokus and Dorothy sat down quite suddenly. The settle had arrived and hit them smartly behind the knees. The Cowardly Lion dodged just in time and lay down with a growl beside it.

"Now that you're settled," began the King in a resigned voice, "we might try again. What is your motto?"

This took even Sir Hokus by surprise, but before he could answer, the King snapped out:

"Come late and stay early! How's that?"

"Very good," said Sir Hokus with a wink at Dorothy.

"Next time, don't come at all," mumbled Sticken Plaster, his mouth full of biscuit.

"And you wanted?" the King asked uneasily.

"Dinner for three," said the Knight promptly and with another bow.

"Now that's talking." The King looked admiringly at Sir Hokus. "This Little With D had matters all tangled up. One time at a thing! That's my motto!"

Leaning over, the King pressed another button. By this time, the Fixes had lost interest in the visitors and went calmly on with their dinners. Three tables came pattering up, and the settle drew itself up of its own accord. Dorothy placed the Cowardly Lion's dinner on the ground, and then she and Sir Hokus enjoyed the first good meal they had had since they left Pokes. They were gradually becoming used to their strange surroundings.

"You ask him about the Scarecrow," begged Dorothy. Everybody had finished, and the tables were withdrawing in orderly groups. The King was leaning sleepily back in his chair.

"Ahem," began the Knight, rising stiffly, "has your Majesty seen aught of a noble Scarecrow? And could your Supreme Fixity tell us aught—"

The King's eyes opened. "You're out of turn," he interrupted crossly. "We're only to the second question. How will you spend the night?"

"In sleep," answered Sir Hokus promptly, "if your Majesty permits."

"I do," said the King solemnly. "That gets me out of entertaining. Early to bed and late to rise, that's my motto. Next! It's your turn," he added irritably as Sir Hokus did not immediately answer.

"Have you seen aught of the noble Scarecrow?" asked Sir Hokus, and all of them waited anxiously for the King's reply.

"I don't know about the Scarecrow. I've seen a Scarecrow, and a sensible chap he was, hanging still like a reasonable person and letting chairs and tables chase themselves 'round."

"Where was he?" asked Sir Hokus in great agitation.

"In a picture," said the King. "Wait, I'll ring for it."

"No use," said the Knight in a disappointed voice. "We're looking for a man.

"Would you mind telling me why you are all so still, and why all your furniture runs around?" asked Dorothy, who was growing a little restless.

"You forget where you are, and you're out of turn. But I'll overlook it this once," said the King. "Have you ever noticed, Little With D, that furniture lasts longer than people?"

"Why, yes," admitted Dorothy.

"Well, there you are!" King Fix Sit folded his hands and regarded her complacently. "Here we manage things better. We stand still and let the furniture run around and wear itself out. How does it strike you?"

"It seems sensible," acknowledged Dorothy. "But don't you ever grow tired of standing still?"

"I've heard of growing hair and flowers and corn, but never of growing tired. What is it?" asked Sticken Plaster, leaning toward Dorothy.

"I think she's talked enough," said the King, closing his eyes.

Sir Hokus had been staring anxiously at the King for some time. Now he came close to the monarch's side, and standing on tiptoe whispered hoarsely: "Hast any dragons here?"

"Did you say wagons?" asked the King, opening his eyes with a terrible yawn.

"Dragons!" hissed the Knight.

"Never heard of 'em," said the King. The Cowardly Lion chuckled behind his whiskers, and Sir Hokus in great confusion stepped back.

"What time is it?" demanded the King suddenly. He touched a bell, and next minute a whole company of clocks came running down the street. The big ones pushed the little ones, and a grandfather clock ran so fast that it tripped over a cobblestone and fell on its face, which cracked all the way across.

"You've plenty of time; why don't you take it?" called the King angrily, while two clothes trees helped the clock to its feet.

"They're all different," giggled Dorothy, nudging the Cowardly Lion. Some pointed to eight o'clock, some to nine, and others to half past ten.

"Why shouldn't they be different?" asked Sticken haughtily. "Some run faster than others!"

"Pass the time, please," said the King, looking hard at Dorothy.

"The lazy lump!" growled the Cowardly Lion.

But Dorothy picked up the nearest little clock and handed it to King Fix Sit.

"I thought so," yawned the King, pointing at the clock. At this, everybody began ringing bells till Dorothy was obliged to cover her ears. In an instant, the whole street was filled with beds, "rolling up just as if they were taxis," laughed Dorothy to Sir Hokus. The Knight smiled faintly, but as he had never seen a taxi, he could not appreciate Dorothy's remark.

"Here come your beds," said the King shortly. "Tell them to take you around the corner. I can't abide snoring."

"I don't snore, thank you," said Dorothy angrily, but the King had stepped into his bed and drawn the curtains tight.

"We might as well go to bed, I 'spose," said the little girl. "I'm so tired!"

The three beds were swaying restlessly in the middle of the street. They were tall, four-post affairs with heavy chintz hangings. Dorothy chose the blue one, and Sir Hokus lifted her up carefully and then went off to catch his bed, which had gotten into an argument with a lamppost. When he spoke to it sharply, it left off and came trotting over to him. The Cowardly Lion, contrary to his usual custom, leaped into his bed, and soon the three four-posters were walking quietly down the street, evidently following the King's instructions.

Dorothy slipped off her shoes and dress and nestled comfortably down among the soft covers. "Just like sleeping in a train," she thought drowsily. "What a lot I shall have to tell the Scarecrow and Ozma when I get home."

"Good night!" said the bed politely.

"Good night!" said Dorothy, too nearly asleep to even think it strange for a bed to talk. "Good night!"

Chapter 13

Dancing Beds and the Roads that Unrolled

"It must be a shipwreck," thought Dorothy, sitting up in alarm. She seemed to be tossing about wildly.

"Time for little girls to get up," grumbled a harsh voice that seemed to come from the pillows.

Dorothy rubbed her eyes. One of the bedposts was addressing her, and the big four-poster itself was dancing a regular jig.

"Oh, stop!" cried Dorothy, holding on to the post to keep from bouncing out. "Can't you see I'm awake?"

"Well, I go off duty now, and you'll have to hurry," said the bed sulkily. "I'm due at the lecture at nine."

"Lecture?" gasped Dorothy.

"What's so queer about that?" demanded the

bed coldly. "I've got to keep well posted, haven't I? I belong to a polished set, I do. Hurry up, little girl, or I'll throw you out."

"I'm glad my bed doesn't talk to me in this impertinent fashion," thought Dorothy, slipping into her dress and combing her hair with her side comb. "Imagine being ordered about by a bed! I wonder if Sir Hokus is up." Parting the curtains, she jumped down, and the bed, without even saying goodbye, took itself off.

Sir Hokus was sitting on a stile, polishing his armour with a pillowslip he had taken from his bed, and the Cowardly Lion was lying beside him lazily thumping his tail and making fun of the passing furniture.

"Have you had breakfast?" asked Dorothy, joining her friends.

"We were waiting for your Ladyship," chuckled the Cowardly Lion. "Would you mind ordering two for me, Hokus? I find one quite insufficient."

Sir Hokus threw away the pillowslip, and talking cheerfully they walked toward King Fix Sit's circle. The beds had been replaced by breakfast tables, and the whole street was eating busily.

"Good morning, King," said Sir Hokus. "Four

breakfasts, please." The king rang a bell four times without looking up from his oatmeal. Seeing that he did not wish to be disturbed, the three waited quietly for their tables.

"In some ways," said Dorothy, contentedly munching a hot roll, "in some ways this is a very comfortable place."

"In sooth 'tis that," mumbled Sir Hokus, his mouth full of baked apple. As for the Cowardly Lion, he finished his two breakfasts in no time. "And now," said Sir Hokus as the tables walked off, "let us continue our quest. Could'st tell us the way to the Emerald City, my good King Fix?"

"If you go, go away. And if you stay, stay away. That's my motto," answered King Fix shortly. "I can't have people running around here like common furniture," he added in a grieved voice. All the Fix Its nodded vigorously.

"Let them take their stand or their departure," said Sticken Plaster firmly.

The King felt in his pocket and brought out three pieces of chalk. "Go to the end of the street. Choose a place and draw your circle. In five minutes you will find it impossible to move out of the circle, and you will be saved all this unnecessary motion."

"But we don't want to come to a standstill," objected Dorothy.

"No, by my good sword!" spluttered the Knight, glaring around nervously. Then, seeing the King looked displeased, he made a low bow. "If your Highness could graciously direct us out of the city—"

"Buy a piece of road and go where it takes you," snapped the King. Seeing no more was to be got out of him, they started down the long street.

"I wonder what they do when it rains?" said Dorothy, looking curiously at the solemn rows of people.

"Call for roofs, silly!" snapped a Fix, staring at her rudely. "If you would spend your time thinking instead of walking, you'd know more."

"Go to, and swallow a gooseberry!" roared the Knight, waving his sword at the Fix, and Dorothy, fearing an encounter, begged him to come on, which he did—though with many backward glances.

Fix City seemed to consist of one long street, and they had soon come to the very end.

"Uds daggers!" gasped Sir Hokus.

"Great palm trees," roared the Cowardly Lion.

As for Dorothy, she could do nothing but

stare. The street ended surely enough, and beyond there was nothing at all. That is, nothing but air.

"Well," said the Cowardly Lion, backing a few paces, "this is a pretty fix."

"Glad you like it," said a wheezy voice. The three travellers turned in surprise. A huge Fix was regarding them with interest. His circle, which was the last in the row, was about twenty times as large as the other circles, and on the edge stood a big sign:

ROAD SHOP

"Don't you remember, the King said something about buying a road," said Dorothy in an excited undertone to the Knight.

"Can'st direct us to a road, my good man?" asked Sir Hokus with a bow. The Fix jerked his thumb back at the sign. "What kind of a road to you want?" he asked hoarsely.

"A road that will take us back to the Emerald City, please," said Dorothy.

"I can't guarantee anything like that," declared the Fix, shaking his head. "Our roads go where they please, and you'll have to go where they take you. Do you want to go on or off?"

"On," shivered the Cowardly Lion, looking with a shudder over the precipice at the end of the street.

"What kind of a road will you have? Make up your minds, please. I am busy."

"What kind of roads have you?" asked Dorothy timidly. It was her first experience at buying roads, and she felt a bit perplexed.

"Sunny, shady, straight, crooked, and cross-roads," snapped the Fix.

"We wouldn't want a cross one," said Dorothy positively. "Have you any with trees at both sides and water at the end?"

"How many yards?" asked the Fix, taking a pair of shears as large as himself off a long counter beside him.

"Five miles," said Sir Hokus as Dorothy looked confused. "That ought to take us somewhere!"

The Fix rang one of the bells in the counter. The next minute, a big trap door in the ground opened, and a perfectly huge roll bounced out at his feet.

"Get on," commanded the Fix in such a sharp tone that the three jumped to obey. Holding fast to Sir Hokus, Dorothy stepped on the piece of road that had already unrolled. The Cowardly Lion, looking very anxious, followed. No sooner had they done so than the road gave a terrific leap forward that stretched the three flat upon their backs and started unwinding from its spool at a terrifying speed. As it unrolled, tall trees snapped erect on each side and began laughing derisively at the three travellers huddled together in the middle.

"G-g-glad we only took five miles," stuttered Dorothy to the Knight, whose armour was rattling like a Ford.

The Cowardly Lion had wound his tail around a tree and dug his claws into the road, for he had no intention of falling off into nothingness. As for the road, it snapped along at about a mile a minute, and before they had time to grow accustomed to this singular mode of travel, it gave a final jump that sent them circling into the air, and began rapidly winding itself up. Down, down, down whirled Dorothy, falling with a resounding splash into a broad stream of water. Then down, down, down again, almost to the bottom.

"Help!" screamed Dorothy as her head rose above water, and she began striking out feebly. But the fall through the air had taken all her breath.

"What do you want?" A thin, neat little man was watching her anxiously from the bank, making careful notes in a book that he held in one hand.

"Help! Save me!" choked Dorothy, feeling herself going down in the muddy stream again.

"Wait! I'll look it up under the 'H's," called the little man, making a trumpet of his hands. "Are you an island? An island is a body of land entirely surrounded by water, but this seems to be a somebody," Dorothy heard him mutter as he whipped over several pages of his book. "Sorry," he called back, shaking his head slowly, "but this is the wrong day. I only save lives on Monday."

"Stand aside, Mem, you villain!" A second little man exactly like the first except that he was exceedingly untidy plunged into the stream.

"It's no use," thought Dorothy, closing her eyes, for he had jumped in   far below the spot where she had fallen and was making no progress whatever. The waters rushed over her head the second time. Then she felt herself being dragged upward.

When she opened her eyes, the Cowardly Lion was standing over her. "Are you all right?" he rumbled anxiously. "I came as soon as I could. Fell in way upstream. Seen Hokus?"

"Oh, he'll drown," cried Dorothy, forgetting her own narrow escape. "He can't swim in that heavy armour!"

"Never fear, I'll get him," puffed the Cowardly Lion, and without waiting to catch his breath he plunged back into the stream. The little man who only saved lives on Monday now approached timidly. "I'd like to get a statement from you, if you don't mind. It might help me in the future."

"You might have helped me in the present," said Dorothy, wringing out her dress. "You ought to be ashamed of yourself."

"I'll make a note of that," said the little man earnestly. "But how did you feel when you went down?" He waited, his pencil poised over the little book.

"Go away," cried Dorothy in disgust.

"But my dear young lady—"

"I'm not your dear young lady. Oh, dear, why doesn't the Cowardly Lion come back?"

"Go away, Mem." The second little man, dripping wet, came up hurriedly.

"I was only trying to get a little information," grumbled Mem sulkily. "I'm sorry I couldn't swim faster," said the wet little man, approaching Dorothy apologetically.

"Well, thank you for trying," said Dorothy. "Is he your brother? And could you tell me where you are? You're dressed in yellow, so I 'spose it must be somewhere in the Winkie Country."

"Right in both cases," chuckled the little fellow. "My name is Ran and his name is Memo." He jerked his thumb at the retiring twin. "Randum and Memo—see?"

"I think I do," said Dorothy, half closing her eyes. "Is that why he's always taking notes?"

"Exactly," said Ran. "I do everything at Random, and he does everything at memorandum."

"It must be rather confusing," said Dorothy. Then as she caught sight of the Cowardly Lion dragging Sir Hokus, she jumped up excitedly. Ran, however, took one look at the huge beast and then fled, calling for Mem at the top of his voice. And that is the last Dorothy saw of these singular twins.

The Lion dropped Sir Hokus in a limp heap. When Dorothy unfastened his armour, gallons of water rushed out.

"Sho good of—of—you," choked the poor Knight, trying to straighten up.

"Save your breath, old fellow," said the Cowardly Lion, regarding him affectionately.

"Oh, why did I ask for water on the end of the road?" sighed Dorothy. "But, anyway, we're in some part of the Winkie Country."

Sir Hokus, though still spluttering, was beginning to revive. "Yon noble bheast shall be knighted. Uds daggers! That's the shecond time he's shaved my life!" Rising unsteadily, he tottered over to the Lion and struck him a sharp blow on the shoulder. "Rishe, Shir Cowardly Lion," he cried hoarsely, and fell headlong, and before Dorothy or the lion had recovered from their surprise he was fast asleep, mumbling happily of dragons and bludgeons.

"We'll have to wait till he gets rested," said Dorothy. "And until I get dry." She began running up and down, then stopped suddenly before the Lion.

"And there's something else for Professor Wogglebug to put in his book, Sir Cowardly Lion."

"Oh, that!" mumbled the Cowardly Lion, looking terribly embarrassed. "Whoever heard of a Cowardly Knight? Nonsense!"

"No, it isn't nonsense," said Dorothy stoutly. "You're a knight from now on. Won't the Scarecrow be pleased?"

"If we ever find him," sighed the Lion, settling himself beside Sir Hokus.

"We will," said Dorothy gaily. "I just feel it."

Chapter 14

Sons and Grandsons Greet the Scarecrow

Although the Scarecrow had been on Silver Island only a few days, he had already instituted many reforms, and thanks to his cleverness the people were more prosperous than ever before. Cheers greeted him wherever he went, and even old Chew Chew was more agreeable and no longer made bitter remarks to Happy Toko. The Scarecrow himself, however, had four new wrinkles and was exceedingly melancholy. He missed the carefree life in Oz, and every minute that he was not ruling the island he was thinking about his old home and dear, jolly comrades in the Emerald City.

"I almost hope they will look in the Magic Picture and wish me back again," he mused pensively. "But it is my duty to stay here. I have a family to support." So he resolved to put the best face he could on the matter, and Happy Toko did his utmost to cheer up his royal master. The second morning after the great victory, he came running into the silver throne room in a great state of excitement.

"The honourable Offspring have arrived!" announced Happy, turning a somersault. "Come, ancient and amiable Sir, and gaze upon your sons and grandsons!" The Scarecrow sprang joyously from his silver throne, upsetting a bowl of silver fish and three silver vases. At last a real family! Ever since his arrival, the three Princes and their fifteen little sons had been cruising on the royal pleasure barge, so that the Scarecrow had not caught a glimpse of them.

"This is the happiest moment of my life!" he exclaimed, clasping his yellow gloves and watching the door intently. Happy looked a little uneasy, for he knew the three Princes to be exceedingly haughty and overbearing, but he said nothing, and next minute the Scarecrow's family stepped solemnly into the royal presence.

"Children!" cried the Scarecrow, and with his usual impetuousness rushed forward and flung his arms around the first richly clad Prince.

"Take care! Take care, ancient and honourable

papa!" cried the young Silverman, backing away. "Such excitement is not good for one of your advanced years." He drew himself away firmly and, adjusting a huge pair of silver spectacles, regarded the Scarecrow attentively. "Ah, how you have changed!"

"He looks very feeble, Too Fang, but may he live long to rule this flowery island and our humble selves!" said the second Prince, bowing stiffly.

"Do you not find the affairs of state fatiguing, darling papa?" inquired the third Prince, fingering a jewelled chain that hung around his neck.

"I, as your eldest son, shall be delighted to relieve you should you wish to retire. Get back ten paces, you!" he roared at Happy Toko.

The poor Scarecrow had been so taken aback by this cool reception that he just stared in disbelief.

"If the three honourable Princes will retire themselves, I will speak with my grandsons," he said dryly, bowing in his most royal manner. The three Princes exchanged startled glances. Then, with three low salaams, they retired backward from the hall.

"And now, my dears—!" The Scarecrow looked wistfully at his fifteen silken-clad little grandsons. Their silver hair, plaited tightly into little queues, stood out stiffly on each side of their heads and gave them a very curious appearance. At his first word, the fifteen fell dutifully on their noses. As soon as they were right side up, the Scarecrow, beginning at the end of the row, addressed a joking question to each in his most approved Oz style. But over they went again, and answered merely:

"Yes, gracious Grand-papapapah!" or "No honourable Grandpapapapah!" And the constant bobbing up and down and papahing so confused the poor Scarecrow that he nearly gave up the conversation.

"It's no use trying to talk to these children," he wailed in disgust, "they're so solemn. Don't you ever laugh?" he cried in exasperation, for he had told them stories that would have sent the Oz youngsters into hysterics.

"It is not permissible for a Prince to laugh at the remarks of his honourable grandparent," whispered Happy Toko, while the fifteen little Princes banged their heads solemnly on the floor.

"Honourable fiddlesticks!" exclaimed the Scarecrow, slumping back on his throne. "Bring cushions." Happy Toko ran off nimbly, and soon the fifteen little Princes were seated in a circle at the Scarecrow's feet. "To prevent prostrations," said the

Scarecrow.

"Yes, old Grandpapapapapah!" chorused the Princes, bending over as far as they could.

"Wait!" said the Scarecrow hastily, "I'll tell you a story. Once upon a time, to a beautiful country called Oz, which is surrounded on all sides by a deadly desert, there came a little girl named Dorothy. A terrible gale—Well, what's the matter now?" The Scarecrow stopped short, for the oldest Prince had jerked a book out of his sleeve and was flipping over the pages industriously.

"It is not on the map, great Grand papapapah," he announced solemnly, and all of the other little Princes shook their heads and said dully, "Not on the map."

"Not on the map—Oz? Of course it's not. Do you suppose we want all the humans in creation coming there?" Calming down, the Scarecrow tried to continue his story, but every time he mentioned Oz, the little Princes shook their heads stubbornly and whispered, "Not on the map," till the usually good-tempered Scarecrow flew into perfect passion.

"Not on the map, you little villains!" he screamed, forgetting they were his grandsons. "What difference does that make? Are your heads solid silver?"

"We do not believe in Oz," announced the oldest Prince serenely. "There is no such place."

"No such place as Oz—Happy, do you hear that?" The Scarecrow's voice fairly crackled with indignation. "Why, I thought everybody believed in Oz!"

"Perhaps your Highness can convince them later," suggested the Imperial Punster. "This way, offspring." His Master, he felt, had had enough family for one day. So the fifteen little Princes, with fifteen stiff little bows, took themselves back to the royal nursery. As for the Scarecrow, he paced disconsolately up and down his magnificent throne room, tripping over his kimono at every other step.

"You're a good boy, Tappy," said the Scarecrow as Happy returned, "but I tell you being a grandparent is not what I thought it would be. Did you hear them tell me right to my face they did not believe in Oz? And my sons—ugh!"

"Fault of their bringing up," said Happy Toko comfortingly. "If your serene Highness would just tell me more of that illustrious country!" Happy knew that nothing cheered the Scarecrow like talking of Oz, and to tell the truth Happy himself never tired of the Scarecrow's marvellous stories. So the two slipped quietly into the palace gardens, and the Scarecrow related for the fourteenth time the story of his discovery by Dorothy and the story of Ozma, and almost forgot that he was an Emperor.

"Your Highness knows the history of Oz by heart," said Happy admiringly as the Scarecrow paused.

"I couldn't do that," said the Scarecrow gently, "for you see, Happy, I have no heart."

"Then I wish we all had none!" exclaimed Happy Toko, rolling up his eyes. The Scarecrow looked embarrassed, so the little Punster threw back his head and sang a song he had been making up while the Scarecrow had been telling his stories:

"The Scarecrow was standing alone in a field,
Inviting the crows to keep off,
When the straw in his chest began tickling his vest
And he couldn't resist a loud cough.

The noise that was heard so surprised ev'ry bird,
That the flock flew away in a fright,
But the Scarecrow looked pleased, and he said "If I'd
sneezed

It wouldn't have been so polite."

"Ho!" roared the Scarecrow, "You're almost as good at making verses as Scraps, Write that down for me, Tappy. I'd like to show it to her."

"Hush!" whispered Happy, holding up his finger warningly. The Scarecrow turned so suddenly that the silver pigtail pinned to the back of his hat wound itself tightly around his neck. No wonder! On the other side of the hedge the three Princes were walking up and down, conversing in indignant whispers.

"What a horrible shape our honourable Papa has reappeared in. I hear that it never wears out," muttered one. "He may continue just as he is for years and years. How am I ever to succeed him, I'd like to know. Why, he may outlive us all!"

"We might throw him into the silver river," said the second hopefully.

"No use," choked the third. "I was just talking to the Imperial Soothsayer, and he tells me that no one from this miserable Kingdom of Oz can be destroyed. But I have a plan. Incline your Royal ears—listen." The voices dropped to such a low whisper that neither Happy nor the Scarecrow could hear one word.

"Treason!" spluttered Happy, making ready to spring through the hedge, but the Scarecrow seized him by the arm and drew him away.

"I don't believe they like their poor papa," exclaimed the Scarecrow when they were safely back in the throne room. "I'm feeling older than a Kinkajou. Ah, Happy Oko, why did I ever slide down my family tree? It has brought me nothing but unhappiness."

Chapter 15

The Three Princes Plot to Undue the Emperor

"Let me help your Imperial Serenity!"

"Bring a cane!"

"Carefully, now!"

The three royal Princes, with every show of affection, were supporting the Scarecrow to the silver bench in the garden where he usually sat during luncheon.

"Are you quite comfortable?" asked the elder. "Here, Happy, you rogue, fetch a scarf for his Imperial Highness. You must be careful, dear Papa Scarecrow. At your age, drafts are dangerous." The rascally Prince wound the scarf about the Scarecrow's neck.

"What do you suppose they are up to?" asked the Scarecrow, staring after the three suspiciously. "Why this sudden devotion? It upsets my Imperial Serenity a lot."

"Trying to make you feel old," grumbled

Happy. Several hours had passed since they had overheard the conversation in the garden. The Scarecrow had decided to watch his sons closely and fall in with any plan they suggested so they would suspect nothing. Then, when the time came, he would act. Just what he would do he did not know, but his excellent brains would not, he felt sure, desert him. Happy Toko sat as close to the Scarecrow as he could and scowled terribly whenever the Princes approached, which was every minute or so during the afternoon.

"How is the Scarecrow's celestial old head?"

"Does he suffer from honourable gout?"

"Should they fetch the Imperial Doctor?"

The Scarecrow, who had never thought of age in his whole straw life, became extremely nervous.

Was he really old? Did his head ache? When no one was looking, he felt himself carefully all over. Then something of his old time Oz spirit returned. Seizing the cushion that his eldest son was placing at his back, he hurled it over his head. Leaping from his throne, he began turning handsprings in a careless and sprightly manner.

"Don't you worry about your honourable old papa," chuckled the Scarecrow, winking at Happy

Toko. "He's good for a couple of centuries!"

The three Princes stared sourly at this exhibition of youth.

"But your heart," objected the eldest Prince.

"Have none," laughed the Scarecrow. Snatching off the silver cord from around his waist, he began skipping rope up and down the hall. The Princes, tapping their foreheads significantly, retired, and the Scarecrow, throwing his arm around Happy Toko, began whispering in his ear. He had a plan himself. They would see!

Meanwhile, off in his dark cave in one of the silver mountains, the Grand Gheewizard of the Silver Island was stirring a huge kettle of magic. Every few moments he paused to read out of a great yellow book that he had propped up on the mantle. The fire in the huge grate leaped fiercely under the big, black pot, and the sputtering candles on each side of the book sent creepy shadows into the dark cave. Dark chests, books, bundles of herbs, and heaps of gold and silver were everywhere. Whenever the Gheewizard turned his back, a rheumatic silver-scaled old dragon would crawl toward the fire and swallow a mouthful of coals, until the old Gheewizard caught him in the act and chained him to a ring in the corner of the cave.

"Be patient, little joy of my heart! Our fortune is about to be made," hissed the wizened little man, waving a long iron spoon at the dragon. "You shall have a bucket of red-hot coals every hour and I a silver cap with a tassel. Have not the Royal Princes promised it?" The dragon shuffled about and finally went to sleep, smoking sulkily.

"Is it finished, son of a yellow dog?" Through the narrow opening of the cave, the youngest Prince stuck his head.

"I am working as fast as I can, Honourable Prince, but the elixir must boil yet one more night. Tomorrow, when the sun shines on the first bar of your celestial window, come, and all will be ready."

"Are you sure you have found it?" asked the Prince, withdrawing his head, for the smoking dragon and steam from the kettle made him cough.

"Quite sure," wheezed the Grand Gheewizard, and fell to stirring the kettle with all his might.

The Scarecrow, although busy with trials in the great courtroom of the palace, felt that something unusual was in the air. The Princes kept nodding to one another, and the Grand Chew Chew and General Mugwump had their heads together at every opportunity.

"Something's going to happen, Tappy. I feel it in my straw," whispered the Scarecrow as he finished trying the last case. At that very minute, the Grand Chew Chew arose and held up his hand for silence. Everybody paused in their way to the exits and looked with surprise at the old Silverman.

"I have to announce," said the Grand Chew Chew in a solemn voice, "that the Great and Imperial Chang Wang Woe will tomorrow be restored to his own rightful shape. The Grand Gheewizard of the realm has discovered a magic formula to break the enchantment and free him from this distressing Scarecrow body. Behold for the last the Scarecrow of Oz. Tomorrow he will be our old and glorious Emperor!"

"Old and glorious?" gasped the Scarecrow, nearly falling from his throne.

"Tappy! I forgot to lock up the wizards. Great Cornstarch! Tomorrow I will be eighty-five years old."

Such cheers greeted the Grand Chew Chew's announcement that no one even noticed the Scarecrow's distress.

"I, also, have an announcement!" cried the eldest Prince, standing up proudly. "To make the celebration of my royal Papa's restoration complete, we have chosen the lovely and charming Orange Blossom for his bride."

"Bride!" gulped the Scarecrow. "But I do not approve of second marriages. I refuse to—"

No one paid the slightest attention to the Scarecrow's remarks.

"Hold my hand, Tappy," sighed the Scarecrow weakly. "It may be your last chance." Then he sat up and stared in good earnest, for the Prince was leading forward a tall, richly clad lady.

"Orange Blossom!" muttered the Scarecrow under his breath. "He means Lemon Peel! Silver grandmother, Tappy!" Orange Blossom was a cross-looking Princess of seventy-five, at least.

"She is a sister of the King of the Golden Islands," whispered General Mugwump. "Of a richness surpassing your own. Let me felicitate your Highness."

"Fan me, Tappy! Fan me!" gasped the Scarecrow. Then he straightened himself suddenly. The time had come for action. He would say nothing to anyone, but that night he would escape and try to find his way back to Oz, family or no family! He bowed graciously to Princess Orange Blossom, to the Grand Chew Chew, and to his sons.

"Let everything be made ready for the ceremony, and may tomorrow indeed bring me to myself," he repeated solemnly. Nothing was talked of that evening but the Emperor's impending marriage and the Grand Gheewizard's discovery. The Scarecrow seemed the least excited person in the palace. Sitting on his throne, he pretended to read the Royal Silver Journal, but he was really waiting impatiently for the courtiers to retire. Finally, when the last one had bowed himself out and only Happy Toko remained in the throne room, the Scarecrow began making his plans.

"It's no use, Tappy," said he, tying up a few little trinkets for Dorothy in a silk handkerchief, "I'd rather be straw than meat. I'd rather be a plain Scarecrow in Oz than Emperor of the Earth! They may be my sons, but all they want is my death. I'm going back to my old friends. I'd rather—". He got no farther. A huge slave seized him suddenly from behind, while another caught Happy Toko around his fat little waist.

"Tie them fast," said the eldest Prince, smiling wickedly at the Scarecrow. "Here, tie him to the beanstalk. Merely a part of the Grand Gheewizard's formula," he exclaimed maliciously as the struggling Scarecrow was bound securely to his family tree. "Good night, dear papa Scarecrow. Tomorrow you will be your old self again, and in a few short years I will be Emperor of the Silver Islands!"

"This rather upsets our plans, eh Tappy?" wheezed the Scarecrow after a struggle with his bonds.

"Pigs! Weasels!" choked Tappy. "What are we to do?"

"Alas!" groaned the Scarecrow. "Tomorrow there will be no Scarecrow in Oz. What will Dorothy and Ozma think? And once I am changed into my old Imperial self, I can never make the journey to the Emerald City. Eighty-six is too old for traveling."

"Has your Majesty forgotten the wonderful brains given to you by the Wizard of Oz?"

"I had—for a moment," confessed the Scarecrow. "Be quiet, Tappy, while I think." Pressing his head against the magic beanpole, the Scarecrow thought and thought, harder than he had ever done in the course of his adventurous life, and in the great, silent hall Happy Toko struggled to set himself free.

Chapter 16

Dorothy and Her Guardians Meet New Friends

While all these exciting things were happening to the poor Scarecrow, Dorothy, Sir Hokus and the Cowardly Lion had been having adventures of their own. For three days, they had wandered through a deserted part of the Winkie Country, subsisting largely on berries, sleeping under trees, and looking in vain for a road to lead them back to the Emerald City. On the second day, they had encountered an ancient woodsman, too old and deaf to give them any information. He did, however, invite them into his hut and give them a good dinner and a dozen sandwiches to carry away with them.

"But, oh, for a good old pasty!" sighed Sir Hokus late on the third afternoon as they finished the last of the crumbly sandwiches.

"Do you know," said Dorothy, looking through the straggly fields and woods ahead, "I believe we've been going in the wrong direction again." "Again!" choked the Cowardly Lion. "You mean still. I've been in a good many parts of Oz, but this—this is the worst."

"Not even one little dragon!" Sir Hokus shook his head mournfully. Then, seeing that Dorothy was tired and discouraged, he pretended to strum on a guitar and sang in his high-pitched voice:

"A rusty Knight in steel bedite
And Lady Dot, so fair,
Sir Lion bold, with mane of gold
And might besides to spa—ha—hare!
And might beside to spare!
The dauntless three, a company
Of wit and bravery are,
Who seek the valiant Scarecrow man,
Who seek him near and fa—har—har,
Who seek him near and fa—har!"

"Oh, I like that!" cried Dorothy, jumping up and giving Sir Hokus a little squeeze. "Only you should have said trusty Knight."

The Cowardly Lion shook his golden mane. "Let's do a little reconnoitering, Hokus," he said carelessly. He felt he must live up to the song somehow. "Perhaps we'll find a sign."

"I don't believe in signs anymore," laughed Dorothy, "but I'm coming too." Sir Hokus' song had cheered them all, and it wasn't the first time the Knight had helped make the best of a tiresome journey.

"The air seemeth to grow very hot," observed Sir Hokus after they had walked along silently for a time. "Hast noticed it, Sir Cowardly?"

"No, but I've swallowed some of it," coughed the Cowardly Lion, looking suspiciously through the trees.

"I'll just step forward and see what it is," said the Knight. As he disappeared, the truth dawned on Dorothy.

"Wait! Wait! Don't go! Please, please, Sir Hokus, come back, come back!" cried the little girl, running after him as fast as she could.

"What's the matter?" rumbled the Cowardly Lion, thudding behind her. Then both, coming suddenly out of the woods, gave a terrible scream, which so startled Sir Hokus that he fell over backwards. Just in time, too, for another step would have taken him straight on to the Deadly Desert, which destroys every living thing and keeps all intruders away from Oz.

"What befell?" puffed Sir Hokus, getting to his feet. Naturally, he knew nothing of the poisonous sands.

"You did," wheezed the Cowardly Lion in an agitated voice.

"Was it a dragon?" asked the Knight, limping toward them hopefully.

"Sit down!" The Cowardly Lion mopped his brow with his tail. "One step on that desert and it would have been one long goodnight."

"I should say it would!" shuddered Dorothy, and explained to Sir Hokus the deadly nature of the sands. "And do you know what this means?" Dorothy was nearer to tears than even I like to think about. "It means we've come in exactly the wrong direction and are farther away from the Emerald City than we were when we started."

"And seek him near and fa—hah—har," mumbled Sir Hokus with a very troubled light in his kindly blue eyes.

"And seek him near and far."

"Fah—har—har! I should say it was," said the Cowardly Lion bitterly. "But you needn't sing it."

"No, I s'pose not. Uds helmets and hauberks! I s'pose not!" The Knight lapsed into a discouraged silence, and all three sat and stared drearily at the stretch of desert before them and thought gloomily of the rough country behind.

"It's a caravan," wheezed a hoarse voice.

"I doubt that, Camy, I doubt it very much." The shrill nasal voices so startled the three travellers that they swung about in astonishment.

"Great dates and deserts!" burst out the Cowardly Lion, jumping up. And on the whole, this exclamation was entirely suitable, for ambling toward them were a long-legged camel and a wobbly-necked dromedary.

"At last! A steed!" cried the Knight, bounding to his feet.

"I doubt that." The dromedary stopped and looked at him coldly.

"Try me," said the camel amiably. "I'm more comfortable."

"I doubt that, too."

"The doubtful dromedary wept,

As o'er the desert sands he stept,
Association with the sphinx
Has made him doubtful, so he thinks!"

chortled the Knight with his head on one side.

"How did you know?" asked the Dromedary, opening his eyes wide.

"It just occurred to me," admitted Sir Hokus, clearing his throat modestly.

"I doubt that. Somebody told you," said the Doubtful Dromedary bitterly.

"Pon my honour," said Sir Hokus.

"I doubt it, I doubt it very much," persisted the Dromedary, wagging his head sorrowfully.

"You seem to doubt everything!" Dorothy laughed in spite of herself, and the Dromedary regarded her sulkily.

"He does," said the Camel. "It makes him very doubtful company. Now, I like to be comfortable and happy, and you can't be if you're always doubting things and people and places. Eh, my dear?"

"Where did you comfortable and doubtful parties come from?" asked the Cowardly Lion. "Strangers here?"

"Well, yes," admitted the Camel, nibbling the

branch of a tree. "There was a terrific sandstorm, and after blowing and blowing and blowing, we found ourselves in this little wood. The odd part of it is that you talk in our language. Never knew a two-leg to understand a word of Camelia before."

"You're not talking Camelia, you're talking Ozish," laughed Dorothy. "All animals can talk here."

"Well, now, that's very comfortable, I must say," sighed the Camel, "and if you'd just tell me where to go, it would be more comfortable still."

"I doubt that," snapped the Dromedary. "They're no caravan."

"Where do you want to go?" asked the Cowardly Lion, ignoring the Doubtful Dromedary.

"Anywhere, just so we keep moving. We're used to being told when to start and stop, and life is mighty lonely without our Karwan Bashi," sighed the Comfortable Camel.

"Why, I didn't know you smoked!" exclaimed Dorothy in surprise. She thought the camel was referring to a brand of tobacco.

"He means his camel driver," whispered Sir Hokus, eyeing the soft, pillowed seat on the camel's back longingly. Besides the seat, great sacks and bales of goods hung from its sides. The Doubtful

Dromedary was similarly loaded.

"Goodness!" exclaimed Dorothy. A sudden idea had struck her. "You haven't anything to eat in those sacks, have you?"

"Plenty, my child—plenty!" answered the Camel calmly.

"Three cheers for the Comfortable Camel!" roared the Cowardly Lion, while Sir Hokus, following the camel's directions, carefully unfastened a large, woven basket from one of the sacks on its side.

"You may be my Karwan Bashi," announced the Comfortable Camel judiciously as Sir Hokus paused for breath.

"Hear that, Lady Dot?" Sir Hokus swept the camel a bow and fairly beamed with pleasure. Dorothy, meanwhile, had set out an appetizing repast on a small, rocky ledge—a regular feast, it appeared to the hungry travellers. There were loaves of black bread, figs, dates, cheese, and a curious sort of dried meat which the Cowardly Lion swallowed in great quantities.

"Isn't this cosy?" said Dorothy, forgetting the long, weary way ahead. "My, I'm glad we met you!"

"Very comforting to us, too, my dear," said the Camel, swaying complacently. "Isn't it, Doubty?"

"There are some silk cushions in my right-hand saddle sack, but I doubt very much whether you'll like 'em," mumbled the Dromedary gruffly.

"Out with them!" cried Sir Hokus, pouncing on the Doubtful Dromedary, and in a minute each of the party had a cushion and was as snug as possible.

"Could anything have been more fortunate?" exulted the Knight. "We can now resume our journey properly mounted."

"I think I'll ride the Cowardly Lion," said Dorothy, looking uneasily at the high seat on the camel's back. "Let's start before it grows any darker."

They had eaten to heart's content, and now, packing up the remainder of the feast, the little party made ready to start.

Sir Hokus, using the Cowardly Lion as a footstool, mounted the camel, and then Dorothy climbed on her old friend's back, and the little caravan moved slowly through the forest.

"There's a tent in my left-hand saddle sack, but I doubt very much whether you can put it up," said the Doubtful Dromedary, falling in behind the Comfortable Camel. "I doubt it very much indeed."

"How now, what means this doubting?"

called Sir Hokus from his perilous seat. "I'll pitch it when the time comes."

"Mind you don't pitch out when the Camel goes!" called the Cowardly Lion, who would have his little joke. Sir Hokus, to tell the truth, was feeling tossed about and dizzy, but he was too polite to mention the fact. As they proceeded, Dorothy told the Comfortable Camel all about the Scarecrow and Oz.

An occasional word jolted down from above told her that the Knight was singing. They had gone possibly a mile when Dorothy pointed in excitement to a road just ahead.

"We must have missed it before! Wait, I'll see what it's like." Jumping down from the Cowardly Lion's back, she peered curiously at the narrow, tree lined path. "Why, here's a sign!"

"What of?" asked the Comfortable Camel, lurching forward eagerly and nearly unseating the Knight.

WISH WAY

read Dorothy in a puzzled voice.

"Looks like a pretty good road," said the

Comfortable Camel, squinting up its eyes.

"I doubt it, Camy, I doubt it very much," said the Doubtful Dromedary tremulously.

"What does my dear Karwan Bashi think?" asked the Comfortable Camel, looking adoringly back at the Knight.

"It is unwise to go back when the journey lieth forward," said the Knight, and immediately returned to his song. So, single file, the little company turned in at the narrow path, the Comfortable Camel advancing with timid steps and the Doubtful Dromedary bobbing his head dubiously.

Chapter 17

Dorothy and Camy
Vanish into Space

For a short time, everything went well. Then Dorothy, turning to see how Sir Hokus was getting along, discovered that the Doubtful Dromedary had disappeared.

"Why, where in the world?" exclaimed Dorothy. The Comfortable Camel craned his wobbly neck and, when he saw that his friend was gone, burst into tears. His sobs heaved Sir Hokus clear out of his seat and flung him, helmet first, into the dust.

"Go to!" exploded the Knight, sitting up. "If I were a bird, riding in yon nest would be easier." The last of his sentence ended in a hoarse croak. Sir Hokus vanished, and a great raven flopped down in the centre of the road.

"Oh, where is my dear Karwan Bashi? Oh, where is Doubty?" screamed the Comfortable Camel, running around in frenzied circles. "I wish I'd never come on this path!"

"Magic!" gasped Dorothy, clutching the Cowardly Lion's mane. The Comfortable Camel had melted into air before their very eyes.

"I doubt it, I doubt it very much!" coughed a faint voice close to her ear. Dorothy ducked her head involuntarily as a big yellow butterfly settled on the Cowardly Lion's ear.

"Our doubtful friend," whispered the lion weakly. "Oh, be careful, Dorothy dear. We may turn into frogs or something worse any minute."

Dorothy and the Cowardly Lion had had experiences with magic transformations, and the little girl, pressing her fingers to her eyes, tried to think of something to do. The raven was making awkward attempts to fly and cawing "Go to, now!" every other second.

"Oh, I wish dear Sir Hokus were himself again," wailed Dorothy after trying in vain to recall some magic sentences. Presto! The Knight stood before them, a bit breathless from flying, but hearty as ever.

"I see! I see!" said the Cowardly Lion with a little prance. "Every wish you make on this road comes true. Remember the sign: 'Wish Way.'

I wish the Comfortable Camel were back. I wish the Doubtful Dromedary were himself again," muttered the Cowardly Lion rapidly, and in an instant the two creatures were standing in the path.

"Uds bodikins! So I did wish myself a bird!" gasped the Knight, rubbing his gauntlets together excitedly.

"There you are! There you are!" cried the Comfortable Camel, stumbling toward him and resting his foolish head on his shoulder. "Dear, dear Karwan Bashi! And Doubty, old fellow, there you are too! Ah, how comfortable this all is."

"Not two—one," wheezed the Doubtful Dromedary. "And Camy, I doubt very much whether I'd care for butterflying. I just happened to wish myself one!"

"Don't make any more wishes," said the Cowardly Lion sternly.

"Methinks a proper wish might serve us well," observed Sir Hokus. He had been pacing up and down in great excitement. "Why not wish—"

"Oh, stop!" begged Dorothy. "Wait till we've thought it all out. Wishing's awfully particular work!"

"One person better speak for the party," said the Cowardly Lion. "Now, I suggest—"

"Oh, be careful!" screamed Dorothy again. "I wish you would all stop wishing!" Sir Hokus looked at her reproachfully. No wonder. At Dorothy's words, they all found themselves unable to speak. The Doubtful Dromedary's eyes grew rounder and rounder. For the first time in its life, it was unable to doubt anything.

"Now I'll have to do it all," thought Dorothy, and closing her eyes she tried to think of the very best wish for everybody concerned. It was night and growing darker. The Cowardly Lion, the Camel and Dromedary and Sir Hokus peered anxiously at the little girl, wondering what in the world was going to happen. Being wished around is no joke. For five minutes Dorothy thought and thought. Then, standing in the middle of the road, she made her wish in a clear, distinct voice. It was not a very long wish. To be exact, it had only eight words. Eight— short—little words! But stars! No sooner were they out of Dorothy's mouth than the earth opened with a splintering crash and swallowed up the whole company!

Chapter 18

Dorothy Finds the Scarecrow!

The next thing Dorothy knew, she was sitting on the hard floor of a great, dark hall. One lantern burned feebly, and in the dim, silvery light she could just make out the Comfortable Camel scrambling awkwardly to his feet.

"I smell straw," sniffed the Camel softly.

"I doubt very much whether I am going to like this place." The voice of the Doubtful Dromedary came hesitatingly through the gloom.

"By sword and sceptre!" gasped the Knight, "Are you there, Sir Cowardly?"

"Thank goodness, they are!" said Dorothy. Wishing other people about is a risky and responsible business. "They're all here, but I wonder where here is." She jumped up, but at a shuffle of feet drew back.

"Pigs! Weasels!" shrilled an angry voice, and

a fat little man hurled himself at Sir Hokus, who happened to have fallen in the lead.

"Uds trudgeons and bludgeons and maugre thy head!" roared the Knight, shaking him off like a fly.

"Tappy, Tappy, my dear boy. Caution! What's all this?" At the sound of that dear, familiar voice Dorothy's heart gave a skip of joy, and without stopping to explain she rushed forward.

"Dorothy!" cried the Scarecrow, stepping on his kimono and falling off his silvery throne. "Lights, Tappy! More lights, at once!" But Tappy was too busy backing away from Sir Hokus of Pokes.

"Approach, vassal!" thundered the Knight, who under-stood not a word of Tappy's speech. "Approach! I think I've been insulted!" He drew his sword and glared angrily through the darkness, and Tappy, having backed as far as possible, fell heels over pigtail into the silver fountain. At the loud splash, Dorothy hastened to the rescue.

"They're friends, and we've found the Scarecrow, we've found the Scarecrow!" She seized Sir Hokus and shook him till his armour rattled.

"Tappy! Tappy!" called the Scarecrow. "Where in the world did he pagota?" That's exactly what he said, but to Dorothy it sounded like no language at all.

"Why," she cried in dismay, "it's the Scarecrow, but I can't understand a word he's saying!"

"I think he must be talking Turkey," droned the Comfortable Camel, "or donkey! I knew a donkey once, a very uncomfortable party, I—"

"I doubt it's donkey," put in the Dromedary importantly, but no one paid any attention to the two beasts. For Happy Toko had at last dragged himself out of the fountain and set fifteen lanterns glowing.

"Oh!" gasped Dorothy as the magnificent silver throne room was flooded with light, "Where are we?"

The Scarecrow had picked himself up, and with outstretched arms came running toward her talking a perfect Niagara of Silver Islandish.

"Have you forgotten your Ozish so soon?" rumbled the Cowardly Lion reproachfully as Dorothy flung her arms around the Scarecrow. The Scarecrow, seeing the Cowardly Lion for the first time, fairly fell upon his neck. Then he brushed his clumsy hand across his forehead.

"Wasn't I talking Ozish?" he asked in a puzzled voice.

"Oh, now you are!" exclaimed Dorothy. And sure enough, the Scare- crow was talking plain Ozish again. (Which I don't mind telling you is also plain English.)

The Knight had been watching this little reunion with hardly repressed emotion. Advancing hastily, he dropped on one knee.

"My good sword and lance are ever at thy service, my Lord Scarecrow!" he exclaimed feelingly.

"Who is this impulsive person?" gulped the Scarecrow, staring in undisguised astonishment at the kneeling figure of the Sir Hokus of Pokes.

"He's my Knight Errant, and he's taken such good care of me," explained Dorothy eagerly.

"Splendid fellow," hissed the Cowardly Lion in the Scarecrow's other painted ear, "if he does talk odds and ends."

"Any friend of little Dorothy's is my friend," said the Scarecrow, shaking hands with Sir Hokus warmly. "But what I want to know is how you all got here."

"First tell us where we are," begged the little girl, for the Scarecrow's silver hat and queue filled her with alarm.

"You are on the Silver Island," said the

Scarecrow slowly. "And I am the Emperor—or his good-for-nothing spirit—and tomorrow," the Scarecrow glared around wildly, "tomorrow I'll be eighty-five going on eighty-six." His voice broke and ended in a barely controlled sob.

"Doubt that," drawled the Doubtful Dromedary sleepily.

"Eighty-five years old!" gasped Dorothy. "Why, no one in Oz grows any older!"

"We are no longer in Oz." The Scarecrow shook his head sadly. Then, fixing the group with a puzzled stare, he exclaimed, "But how did you get here?"

"On a wish," said the Knight in a hollow voice.

"Yes," said Dorothy, "we've been hunting you all over Oz, and at last we came to Wish Way, and I said 'I wish we were all with the Scarecrow,' just like that—and next minute—"

"We fell and fell—and fell—and fell," wheezed the Comfortable
Camel.

"And fell—and fell—and fell—and fell," droned the Dromedary, "And—"

"Here you are," finished the Scarecrow hastily,

for the Dromedary showed signs of going on forever.

"Now tell us every single thing that has happened to you," demanded Dorothy eagerly.

Happy Toko had recognized Dorothy and the Cowardly Lion from the Scarecrow's description, and he now approached with an arm full of cushions. These he set in a circle on the floor, with one for the Scarecrow in the centre, and with a warning finger on his lips placed himself behind his Master.

"Tappy is right!" exclaimed the Scarecrow. "We must be as quiet as possible, for a great danger hangs over me."

Without more ado, he told them of his amazing fall down the beanstalk; of his adventures on Silver Island; of his sons and grandsons and the Gheewizard's elixir which would turn him from a lively Scarecrow into an old, old Emperor. All that I have told you, he told Dorothy, up to the very point where his eldest son had bound him to the bean pole and tied up poor, faithful Happy Toko. Happy, it seems, had at last managed to free himself, and they were about to make their escape when Dorothy and her party had fallen into the throne room. The Comfortable Camel and Doubtful Dromedary listened politely at first, but worn out by their exciting adventures, fell asleep in the middle of the story.

Nothing could have exceeded Dorothy's dismay to learn that the jolly Scarecrow of Oz, whom she had discovered herself, was in reality Chang Wang Woe, Emperor of Silver Island.

"Oh, this spoils everything!" wailed the little girl. (The thought of Oz without the Scarecrow was unthinkable.) "It spoils everything! We were going to adopt you and be your truly family. Weren't we?"

The Cowardly Lion nodded. "I was going to be your cousin," he mumbled in a choked voice, "but now that you have a family of your own—" The lion miserably slunk down beside Dorothy.

Sir Hokus looked fierce and rattled his sword, but he could think of nothing that would help them out of their trouble.

"To-morrow there won't be any Scarecrow in Oz!" wailed Dorothy. "Oh, dear! Oh, dear!" And the little girl began to cry as if her heart would break.

"Stop! Stop!" begged the Scarecrow, while Sir Hokus awkwardly patted Dorothy on the back. "I'd rather have you for my family any day. I don't care a Kinkajou for being Emperor, and as for my sons, they are unnatural villains who make my life miserable by telling me how old I am!"

"Just like a poem I once read," said Dorothy, brightening up:

"You are old, Father William," the young man said,
"And your hair has become very white,
And yet you incessantly stand on your head!
Do you think, at your age, it is right?"

"That's it, that's it exactly!" exclaimed the Scarecrow as Dorothy finished repeating the verse. "'You are old, Father Scarecrow!' That's all I hear. I did stand on my head, too. And Dorothy, I can't seem to get used to being a grandparent," added the Scarecrow in a melancholy voice. "It's turning my straws grey." He plucked several from his chest and held them out to her. "Why, those little villains don't even believe in Oz! 'It's not on the map, old Grand-papapapapah!'" he mumbled, imitating the tones of his little grandsons so cleverly that Dorothy laughed in spite of herself.

"This is what becomes of pride!" The Scarecrow extended his hands expressively. "Most people who hunt up their family trees are in for a fall, and I've had mine."

"But who do you want to be?" asked the

Knight gravely. "A Scarecrow in Oz—or the—er—Emperor that you were?"

"I don't care who I were!" In his excitement, the Scarecrow lost his grammar completely. "I want to be who I am. I want to be myself."

"But which one?" asked the Cowardly Lion, who was still a bit confused.

"Why, my best self, of course," said the Scarecrow with a bright smile. The sight of his old friends had quite restored his cheerfulness. "I've been here long enough to know that I am a better Scarecrow than an Emperor."

"Why, how simple it is!" sighed Dorothy contentedly. "Professor Wogglebug was all wrong. It's not what you were, but what you are—it's being yourself that counts."

"By my Halidom, the little maid is right!" said Sir Hokus, slapping his knee in delight. "Let your Gheewizard but try his transformations! Out on him! But what says yon honest henchman?" Happy Toko, although he understood no word of the conversation, had been watching the discussion with great interest. He had been trying to attract the Scarecrow's attention for some time, but the Knight was the only one who had noticed him.

"What is it, Tappy?" asked the Scarecrow, dropping easily back into Silver Islandish.

"Honoured Master, the dawn approaches and with it the Royal Princes and the Grand Gheewizard—and your bride!" Happy paused significantly. The Scarecrow shuddered.

"Let's go back to Oz!" said the Cowardly Lion uneasily.

The Scarecrow was feeling in the pocket of his old Munchkin suit which he always wore under his robes of state. "Here!" said he, giving a little pill to Happy Toko. "It's one of Professor Wogglebug's language pills," he exclaimed to Dorothy, "and will enable him to speak and understand Ozish." Happy swallowed the pill gravely.

"Greetings, honourable Ozites!" he said politely as soon as the pill was down. Dorothy clapped her hands in delight, for it was so comfortable to have him speak their own language.

"I could never have stood it here without Tappy Oko!" The Scarecrow looked fondly at his Imperial Punster.

"Queer name he has," rumbled the Cowardly Lion, looking at Happy Toko as if he had thoughts of eating him.

"Methinks he should be knighted," rumbled Sir Hokus, beaming on the little Silverman. "Rise, Sir Pudding!"

"The sun will do that in a minute or more, and then, then we shall all be thrown into prison!" wailed Happy Toko dismally.

"We were going to escape in a small boat," explained the Scarecrow, "but—" It was not necessary for him to finish. A boat large enough to hold Dorothy, the Cowardly Lion, the Scarecrow, Happy Toko, the camel and the dromedary could not very well be launched in secret.

"Oh, dear!" sighed Dorothy, "If I'd only wished you and all of us back in the Emerald City!"

"You wished very well, Lady Dot," said the Knight. "When I think of what I was going to wish for—"

"What were you going to wish, Hokus?" asked the Cowardly Lion curiously.

"For a dragon!" faltered the Knight, looking terribly ashamed.

"A dragon!" gasped Dorothy. "Why, what good would that have done us?"

"Wait!" interrupted the Scarecrow. "I have thought of something! Why not climb my family tree? It is a long, long way, but at the top lies Oz!"

"Grammercy, a pretty plan!" exclaimed Sir Hokus, peering up at the bean pole.

"Wouldn't that be social climbing?" chuckled Happy Toko, recovering his spirits with a bound. The Cowardly Lion said nothing, but heaved a mighty sigh which no one heard, for they were all running toward the bean pole. It was a good family tree to climb, sure enough, for there were handy little notches in the stalk.

"You go first!" Sir Hokus helped Dorothy up. When she had gone a few steps, the Scarecrow, holding his robes carefully, followed, then honest Happy Toko.

"I'll go last," said Sir Hokus bravely, and had just set his foot on the first notch when a hoarse scream rang through the hall.

Chapter 19

Planning to Fly from Silver Island

I t was the Comfortable Camel. Waking suddenly, he found himself deserted. "Oh, where is my dear Karwan Bashi?" he roared dismally. "Come back! Come back!"

"Hush up, can't you?" rumbled the Cowardly Lion. "Do you want Dorothy and everybody to be thrown into prison on our account? We can't climb the bean pole and will have to wait here and face it out."

"But how uncomfortable," wailed the camel. He began to sob heavily. Dorothy, although highest up the bean pole, heard all of this distinctly. "Oh," she cried remorsefully, "we can't desert the Cowardly Lion like this. I never thought about him."

"Spoken like the dear little Maid you are," said the Knight. "The good beast never reminded us of it, either. There's bravery for you!"

"Let us descend at once, I'll not move a step without the Cowardly Lion!" In his agitation, the Scarecrow lost his balance and fell headlong to the ground, knocking Sir Hokus's helmet terribly askew as he passed. The others made haste to follow him and were soon gathered gravely at the foot of the beanstalk.

"I'll have to think of some other plan," said the Scarecrow, looking nervously at the sky, which showed, through the long windows, the first streaks of dawn. The Comfortable Camel controlled its sobs with difficulty and pressed as close to Sir Hokus as it could. The Doubtful Dromedary was still asleep.

"It would have been a terrible climb," mused the Scarecrow, thinking of his long, long fall down the pole. "Ah, I have it!"

"What?" asked Dorothy anxiously.

"I wonder I did not think of it before. Ah, my brains are working better! I will abdicate," exclaimed the Scarecrow triumphantly. "I will abdicate, make a farewell speech, and return with you to Oz!"

"What if they refuse to let your radiant Highness go?" put in Happy Toko tremulously. "What if the Gheewizard should work his magic before you finished your speech?"

"Then we'll make a dash for it!" said Sir Hokus, twirling his sword recklessly.

"I'm with you," said the Cowardly Lion huskily, "but you needn't have come back for me."

"All right!" said the Scarecrow cheerfully. "And now that everything's settled so nicely, we might as well enjoy the little time left. Put out the lights, Tappy. Dorothy and I will sit on the throne, and the rest of you come as close as possible."

Sir Hokus wakened the Doubtful Dromedary and pulled and tugged it across the hall, where it immediately fell down asleep again. The Comfortable Camel ambled about eating the flowers out of the vases. The Cowardly Lion had placed himself at Dorothy's feet, and Sir Hokus and Happy Toko seated themselves upon the first step of the gorgeous silver throne.

Then, while they waited for morning, Dorothy told the Scarecrow all about the Pokes and Fix City, and the Scarecrow told once again of his victory over the king of the Golden Islands.

"Where is the magic fan now?" asked Dorothy at the end of the story. The Scarecrow smiled broadly, and feeling in a deep pocket brought out the little fan and also the parasol he had plucked from the beanstalk. "Do you know," he said smiling, "so much has happened I haven't thought of them since the battle. I was saving them for you, Dorothy."

"For me!" exclaimed the little girl in delight. "Let me see them!" The Scarecrow handed them over obligingly, but Happy Toko trembled so violently that he rolled down the steps of the throne.

"I beg of you!" He scrambled to his feet and held up his hands in terror. "I beg of you, don't open that fan!"

"She's used to magic, Tappy. You needn't worry," said the Scarecrow easily.

"Of course I am," said Dorothy with great dignity. "But this'll be mighty useful if anyone tries to conquer Oz again. We can just fan 'em away."

Dorothy pulled a hair from the Cowardly Lion's mane, and winding it around the little fan, put it carefully in the pocket of her dress. The parasol she hung by its ribbon to her arm.

"Perhaps Ozma will look in the Magic Picture and wish us all back again," said the little girl after they had sat for a time in silence.

"I doubt it." The Dromedary stirred and mumbled in its sleep. "Singular beast, that!" ejaculated the Knight. "Doubting never gets one anywhere."

"Hush!" warned the Scarecrow. "I hear footsteps!" "Come here." Sir Hokus called hoarsely to the camel, who was eating a paper lantern at the other end of the room. The beast ran awkwardly over to the throne, and swallowing the lantern with a convulsive gulp, settled down beside the dromedary.

"Whatever happens, we must stick together," said the Knight emphatically. "Ah—!"

Dorothy held fast to the Scarecrow with one hand and to the throne with the other. The sun had risen at last. There was a loud crash of drums and trumpets, a rush of feet, and into the hall marched the most splendid company Dorothy had seen in her whole life of adventures.

Chapter 20

Dorothy Upsets the Ceremony of the Island

"**A** caravan!" whistled the comfortable Camel, lurching to his feet. "How nice!"

"I doubt that!" The dromedary's eyes flew open, and he stared sleepily at the magnificent procession of Silver Islanders.

First came the musicians, playing their shining silver trumpets and flutes. The Grand Chew Chew and General Mugwump followed, attired in brilliant silk robes of state. Then came the three Princes, glittering with jewelled chains and medals, and the fifteen little Princes, like so many silver butterflies in their satin kimonos. Next appeared a palanquin bearing the veiled Princess Orange Blossom, followed by a whole company of splendid courtiers and after them as many of the everyday Silver Islanders as the hall would hold. There was a moment of silence. Then the whole assemblage, contrary to the Scarecrow's edict, fell upon their faces.

"My!" exclaimed Dorothy, impressed in spite of herself. "Are you sure you want to give up all this?"

"Great Emperor, beautiful as the sun, wise as the stars, and radiant as the clouds, the Ceremony of Restoration is about to begin!" quavered the Grand Chew Chew, rising slowly. Then he paused, for he was suddenly confused by the strange company around the Scarecrow's throne.

"Treachery!" hissed the eldest Prince to the others. "We left him tied to the bean pole. Ancient Papa Scarecrow needs watching! Who are these curious objects he has gathered about him, pray?"

Now by some magic which even I cannot explain, the people from Oz found they could understand all that was being said. When Dorothy heard herself called an object and saw the wicked faces of the three Princes and the stupid little grandsons, she no longer wondered at the Scarecrow's decision.

The Scarecrow himself bowed calmly. "First," said he cheerfully, "let me introduce my friends and visitors from Oz."

The Silver Islanders, who really loved the

Scarecrow, bowed politely as he called out the names of Dorothy and the others. But the three Silver Princes scowled and whispered indignantly among themselves.

"I am growing very wroth!" choked Sir Hokus to the Cowardly Lion. "Let the ceremony proceed!" called the eldest Prince harshly, before the Scarecrow had finished his introductions. "Let the proper body of his Serene Highness be immediately restored. Way for the Grand Gheewizard! Way for the Grand Gheewizard!"

"One moment," put in the Scarecrow in a dignified voice. "I have something to say." The Silver Islanders clapped loudly at this, and Dorothy felt a bit reassured. Perhaps they would listen to reason after all and let the Scarecrow depart peacefully. How they were ever to escape if they didn't, the little girl could not see.

"My dear children," began the Scarecrow in his jolly voice, "nothing could have been more wonderful than my return to this lovely island, but in the years I have been away from you I have changed very much, and I find I no longer care for being Emperor. So with your kind permission, I will keep the excellent body I now have and will abdicate in favour of my eldest son and return with my friends to Oz. For in Oz I really belong."

A dead silence followed the Scarecrow's speech—then perfect pandemonium.

"No! No! You are a good Emperor! We will not let you go!" shrieked the people. "You are our honourable little Father. The Prince shall be Emperor after you have peacefully returned to your ancestors, but not now. No! No! We will not have it!"

"I feared this!" quavered Happy Toko.

"It is not the Emperor, but the Scarecrow who speaks!" shrilled the Grand Chew Chew craftily. "He knows not what he says. But after the transformation—Ah, you shall see!"

The company calmed down at this. "Let the ceremony proceed! Way for the Grand Gheewizard!" they cried exultantly.

"Chew Chew," wailed the Scarecrow, "you're off the track!" But it was too late. No one would listen.

"I'll have to think of something else," muttered the Scarecrow, sinking dejectedly back on his throne.

"Oh!" shuddered Dorothy, clutching the Scarecrow, "Here he comes!"

"Way for the Grand Gheewizard! Way for the Grand Gheewizard!"

The crowd parted. Hobbling toward the throne came the ugly little Gheewizard of the Silver Island holding a large silver vase high above his head, and after him—!

When Sir Hokus caught a glimpse of what came after, he leaped clean over the Comfortable Camel.

"Uds daggers!" roared the Knight. "*At last!*" He rushed forward violently. There was a sharp thrust of his good sword, then an explosion like twenty giant firecrackers in one, and the room became quite black with smoke. Before anyone realized what had happened, Sir Hokus was back, dragging something after him and shouting exuberantly, "A dragon! I have slain a dragon! What happiness!"

Everyone was coughing and spluttering from the smoke, but as it cleared Dorothy saw that it was indeed a dragon Sir Hokus had slain, the rheumatic dragon of the old Gheewizard himself.

"Why didn't you get the wizard?" rumbled the Cowardly Lion angrily. "Must have exploded," said the Comfortable Camel, sniffing the skin daintily.

"Treason!" yelled the three Princes, while the

Grand Gheewizard flung himself on the stone floor and began tearing strand after strand from his silver pigtail.

"He has killed the little joy of my hearth!" screeched the old man. "I will turn him to a cat, a miserable yellow cat, and roast him for dinner!"

"Oh!" cried Dorothy, looking at Sir Hokus sorrowfully. "How could you?"

The slaying of the dragon had thrown the whole hall into utmost confusion. Sir Hokus turned a little pale under his armour, but faced the angry mob without flinching.

"Oh, my dear Karwan Bashi, this is so uncomfortable!" wheezed the camel, glancing back of him with frightened eyes.

"There's a shiny dagger in my left-hand saddlesack. I doubt very much whether they would like it," coughed the Doubtful Dromedary, pressing close to the Knight.

"On with the ceremony!" cried the eldest Prince, seeing that the excitement was giving the Scarecrow's friends too much time to think. "The son of an iron pot shall be punished later!"

"That's right!" cried a voice from the crowd. "Let the Emperor be restored!"

"I guess it's all over," gulped the Scarecrow. "Give my love to Ozma and tell her I tried to come back."

In helpless terror, the little company watched the Gheewizard approach. One could fight real enemies, but magic! Even Sir Hokus, brave as he was, felt that nothing could be done.

"One move and you shall be so many prunes," shrilled the angry old man, fixing the people from Oz with his wicked little eyes. The great room was so still you could have heard a pin drop. Even the Doubtful Dromedary had not the heart to doubt the wizard's power, but stood rigid as a statue.

The wizard advanced slowly, holding the sealed vase carefully over his head. The poor Scarecrow regarded it with gloomy fascination. One more moment and he would be an old, old Silverman. Better to be lost forever! He held convulsively to Dorothy.

As for Dorothy herself, she was trembling with fright and grief. When the Grand Gheewizard raised the vase higher and higher and made ready to hurl it at the Scarecrow, disregarding his dire threat she gave a shrill scream and threw up both hands.

"Great grandmothers!" gasped the Scarecrow,

jumping to his feet. As Dorothy had thrown up her arms, the little parasol swinging at her wrist had jerked open. Up, up, up, and out through the broken skylight in the roof sailed the little Princess of Oz!

The Grand Gheewizard, startled as anyone, failed to throw the vase. Every neck was craned upward, and everyone was gasping with astonishment.

The oldest Prince, as usual, was the first to recover. "Don't stand staring like an idiot! Now's your chance!" he hissed angrily in the Gheewizard's ear.

"I didn't come here to be harried and hurried by foreigners," sobbed the little man. "How is one to work magic when interrupted every other minute? I want my little dragon."

"Oh, come on now, just throw it. I'll get you another dragon," begged the Prince, his hands trembling with excitement.

In the face of this new disaster, the Scarecrow had forgotten all about the Gheewizard. He and the Cowardly Lion and Sir Hokus were running distractedly around the great throne trying to think up a way to rescue Dorothy. As for the Doubtful Dromedary, he was doubting everything in a loud, bitter voice, while the Comfortable Camel fairly snorted with sorrow.

"There! Now's your chance," whispered the Prince. The Scarecrow, with his back to the crowd, was gesturing frantically.

Taking a firm hold on the neck of the vase and with a long incantation which there is no use at all in repeating, the Gheewizard flung the bottle straight at the Scarecrow's head. But scarcely had it left his hand before there was a flash and a flutter and down came Dorothy and the magic parasol right on top of the vase.

Zip! The vase flew in quite another direction, and next minute had burst over the luckless heads of the three plotting Princes, while Dorothy floated gently to earth.

Sir Hokus embraced the Scarecrow, and the Scarecrow hugged the Cowardly Lion, and I don't wonder at all. For no sooner had the magic elixir touched the Princes, than two of them became silver pigs and the eldest a weasel. They had been turned to their true shapes instead of the Scarecrow. And while the company hopped about in alarm, they ran squealing from the hall and disappeared in the gardens.

"Seize the Gheewizard and take him to his cave," ordered the Scarecrow, asserting his authority for the first time since the proceedings has started. He had noticed the old man making queer signs and passes toward Sir Hokus. A dozen took hold of the struggling Gheewizard and hurried him out of the hall.

Sir Hokus, at the request of the Scarecrow, clapped his iron gauntlets for silence.

"You will agree with me, I'm sure," said the Scarecrow in a slightly unsteady voice, "that magic is a serious matter to meddle with. If you will all return quietly to your homes, I will try to find a way out of our difficulties."

The Silver Islanders listened respectfully and after a little arguing among themselves backed out of the throne room. To tell the truth, they were anxious to spread abroad the tale of the morning's happenings.

Princess Orange Blossom, however, refused to depart. Magic or no magic, she had come to marry the Emperor, and she would not leave till the ceremony had been performed.

"But my dear old Lady, would you wish to marry a Scarecrow?" coaxed the Emperor.

"All men are Scarecrows," snapped the Princess sourly.

"Then why marry at all?" rumbled the Cowardly Lion, making a playful leap at her palanquin. This was too much. The Princess swooned on the spot, and the Scarecrow, taking advantage of her unconscious condition, ordered her chair bearers to carry her away as far and as fast as they could run.

"Now," said the Scarecrow when the last of the company had disappeared, "let us talk this over."

Chapter 21

The Escape for the Silver Island

"Well!" gasped Dorothy, fanning herself with her hat, "I never was so s'prised in my life!"

"Nor I," exclaimed the Scarecrow. "The Grand Gheewizard will be suing you for parassault and battery. But how did it happen?"

"Well," began Dorothy, "as soon as the parasol opened, I flew up so fast that I could hardly breathe. Then, after I'd gone ever so far, it came to me that if the parasol went up when it was up, it would come down when it was down. I couldn't leave you all in such a fix—so I closed it, and—"

"Came down!" finished the Scarecrow with a wave of his hand. "You always do the right thing in the right place, my dear."

"It was lucky I hit the vase, wasn't it?" sighed

Dorothy. "But I'm rather sorry about the Princes."

"Served 'em right," growled the Cowardly Lion. "They'll make very good pigs!"

"But who's to rule the island?" demanded Sir Hokus, turning his gaze reluctantly from the smoking dragon skin.

"This will require thought," said the Scarecrow pensively. "Let us all think."

"I doubt that I can ever think again." The Doubtful Dromedary wagged his head from side to side in a dazed fashion.

"Just leave it to our dear Karwan Bashi." The Comfortable Camel nodded complacently at the Knight and began plucking sly wisps from the Scarecrow's boot top. For a short time there was absolute silence. Then Sir Hokus, who had been thinking tremendously with his elbows on his knees, burst out, "Why not Sir Pudding, here? Why not this honest Punster? Who but Happy Toko deserves the throne?"

"The very person!" cried the Scarecrow, clasping his yellow gloves, and taking off his silver hat, he set it impulsively upon the head of the fat little Silver Islander.

"He'll make a lovely Emperor," said Dorothy.

"He's so kind-hearted and jolly. And now the Scarecrow can abdicate and come home to Oz."

They all looked triumphantly at the Imperial Punster, but Happy Toko, snatching off the royal hat, burst into tears.

"Don't leave me behind, amiable Master!" he sobbed disconsolately. "Oh, how I shall miss you!"

"But don't you see," coaxed Dorothy, "the Scarecrow needs you here more than anyplace, and think of all the fine clothes you will have and how rich you will be!"

"And Tappy, my dear boy," said the Scarecrow, putting his arm around Happy Toko, "you might not like Oz any more than I like Silver Island. Then think—if everything goes well, you can visit me— just as one Emperor visits another!"

"And you won't forget me?" sniffed Happy, beginning to like the idea of being Emperor.

"Never!" cried the Scarecrow with an impressive wave.

"And if anything goes wrong, will you help me out?" questioned Happy uncertainly.

"We'll look in the Magic Picture of Oz every month," declared Dorothy, "and if you need us we'll surely find some way to help you."

"An' you ever require a trusty sword, Odds Bodikins!" exclaimed Sir Hokus, pressing Tappy's hand, "I'm your man!"

"All right, dear Master!" Happy slowly picked up the Imperial hat and set it sideways on his head. "I'll do my best."

"I don't doubt it at all," said the Doubtful Dromedary to everyone's surprise.

"Three cheers for the Emperor! Long live the Emperor of the Silver Island," rumbled the Cowardly Lion, and everybody from Oz, even the camel and dromedary, fell upon their knees before Happy Toko.

"You may have my bride, too, Tappy," chuckled the Scarecrow with a wink at Dorothy. "And Tappy," he asked, sobering suddenly, "will you have my grandsons brought up like real children? Just as soon as I return, I shall send them all the Books of Oz."

Happy bowed, too confused and excited for speech.

"Now," said the Scarecrow, seizing Dorothy's hand, "I can return to Oz with an easy mind."

"Doubt that," said the Doubtful Dromedary.

"You needn't!" announced Dorothy. "I've thought it all out." In a few short sentences she outlined her plan.

"Bravo!" roared the Cowardly Lion, and now the little party began in real earnest the preparation for the journey back to Oz. First, Happy brought them a delicious luncheon, with plenty of twigs and hay for the camel and dromedary and meat for the Cowardly Lion. The Scarecrow packed into the camel's sacks a few little souvenirs for the people of Oz. Then they dressed Happy Toko in the Scarecrow's most splendid robe and ordered him to sit upon the throne. Next, the Scarecrow rang for one of the palace servants and ordered the people of the Silver Islands to assemble in the hall.

Presently the Silvermen began to come trooping in, packing the great throne room until it could hold no more. Everyone was chattering excitedly.

It was quite a different company that greeted them. The Scarecrow, cheerful and witty in his old Munchkin suit, Dorothy and Sir Hokus smiling happily, and the three animal members of the party fairly blinking with contentment.

"This," said the Scarecrow pleasantly when everyone was quiet, "is your new Emperor, to whom I ask you to pledge allegiance." He waved proudly in the direction of Happy Toko, who, to tell the truth, presented a truly royal appearance. "It is not possible for me to remain with you, but I shall always watch over this delightful island and with the magic fan vanquish all its enemies and punish all offenders."

Happy Toko bowed to his subjects.

The Silver Islanders exchanged startled glances, then, as the Scarecrow carelessly lifted the fan, they fell prostrate to the earth.

"Ah!" said the Scarecrow with a broad wink at Happy. "This is delightful. You agree with me, I see. Now then, three cheers for Tappy Oko, Imperial Emperor of the Silver Island."

The cheers were given with a will, and Happy in acknowledgement made a speech that has since been written into the Royal Book of state as a masterpiece of eloquence.

Having arranged affairs so satisfactorily, the Scarecrow embraced Happy Toko with deep emotion. Dorothy and Sir Hokus shook hands with him and wished him every success and happiness. Then the little party from Oz walked deliberately to the bean pole in the centre of the hall.

The Silver Islanders were still a bit dazed by the turn affairs had taken and stared in astonishment as the Scarecrow and Sir Hokus fastened thick ropes around the Cowardly Lion, the Doubtful Dromedary and the Comfortable Camel. Similar ropes they tied around their own waists and Dorothy's, and the ends of all were fastened securely to the handle of the magic parasol, which Dorothy held carefully.

"Goodbye, everybody!" called the little girl, suddenly opening the parasol.

"Goodbye!" cried the genial Scarecrow, waving his hand. Too stupefied for speech, the assemblage gaped with amazement as the party floated gently upward. Up—up—and out of sight whirled the entire party.

Chapter 22

The Flight of the Parasol

Holding the handle of the parasol, Dorothy steered it with all the skill of an aviator, and in several minutes after their start the party had entered the deep, black passage down which the Scarecrow had fallen. Each one of the adventurers was fastened to the parasol with ropes of different length so that none of them bumped together, but even with all the care in the world it was not possible to keep them from bumping the sides of the tube. The Comfortable Camel grunted plaintively from time to time, and Dorothy could hear the Doubtful Dromedary complaining bitterly in the darkness. It was pitch dark, but by keeping one hand in touch with the bean pole, Dorothy managed to hold the parasol in the centre.

"How long will it take?" she called breathlessly to the Scarecrow, who was dangling just below.

"Hours!" wheezed the Scarecrow, holding

fast to his hat. "I hope none of the parties on this line hear us," he added nervously, thinking of the Middlings.

"What recks it?" blustered Sir Hokus. "Hast forgotten my trusty sword?" But his words were completely drowned in the rattle of his armour.

"Hush!" warned the Scarecrow, "Or we'll be pulled in." So for almost an hour, they flew up the dark, chimney-like tube with only an occasional groan as one or another scraped against the rough sides of the passage. Then, before they knew what was happening, the parasol crashed into something, half closed, and the whole party started to fall head over heels over helmets.

"O!" gasped Dorothy, turning a complete somersault, "catch hold of the bean pole, somebody!"

"Put up the parasol!" shrieked the Scarecrow. Just then Dorothy, finding herself right side up, grasped the pole herself and snapped the parasol wide open. Up, up, up they soared again, faster than ever!

"We're flying up much faster than I fell down. We must be at the top!" called the Scarecrow hoarsely, "and somebody has closed the opening!"

Chapter 23

Safe at Last in the Land of Oz

"Must we keep bumping until we bump through?" panted Dorothy anxiously.

"No, by my hilts!" roared Sir Hokus, and setting his foot in a notch of the beanstalk, he cut with his sword the rope that bound him to the parasol.

"Put the parasol down half way, and I'll climb ahead and cut an opening."

With great difficulty Dorothy partially lowered the parasol, and instantly their speed diminished. Indeed, they barely moved at all, and the Knight had soon passed them on his climb to the top.

"Are you there?" rumbled the Cowardly Lion anxiously. A great clod of earth landed on his head, filling his eyes and mouth with mud.

"Ugh!" roared the lion.

"It's getting light! It's getting light!" screamed Dorothy, and in her excitement snapped the parasol up.

Sir Hokus, having cut with his sword a large circular hole in the thin crust of earth covering the tube, was about to step out when the parasol, hurling up from below, caught him neatly on its top, and out burst the whole party and sailed up almost to the clouds!

"Welcome to Oz!" cried Dorothy, looking down happily on the dear familiar Munchkin landscape.

"Home at last!" exulted the Scarecrow, wafting a kiss downward. "Let's get down to earth before we knock the sun into a cocked hat," gasped the Cowardly Lion, for Dorothy, in her excitement, had forgotten to lower the parasol.

Now the little girl lowered the parasol carefully at first, then faster and faster and finally shut it altogether.

Sir Hokus took a high dive from the top. Down tumbled the others, over and over. But fortunately for all, there was a great haystack below, and upon this they landed in a jumbled heap close to the magic bean pole. As it happened, there was no one in sight. Up they jumped in a trice, and while the Comfortable Camel and Doubtful Dromedary munched contentedly at the hay, Sir Hokus and the Scarecrow placed some loose boards over the opening around the bean pole and covered them with dirt and cornstalks.

"I will get Ozma to close it properly with the Magic Belt," said the Scarecrow gravely. "It wouldn't do to have people sliding down my family tree and scaring poor Tappy. As for me, I shall never leave Oz again!"

"I hope not," growled the Cowardly Lion, tenderly examining his scratched hide.

"But if you hadn't, I'd never have had such lovely adventures or found Sir Hokus and the Comfortable Camel and Doubtful Dromedary," said Dorothy. "And what a lot I have to tell Ozma! Let's go straight to the Emerald City."

"It's quite a journey," explained the Scarecrow to Sir Hokus, who was cleaning off his armour with a handful of straw.

"I go where Lady Dot goes," replied the Knight, smiling affectionately at the little girl and straightening the ragged hair ribbon which he still wore on his arm.

"Don't forget me, dear Karwan Bashi," wheezed the Comfortable Camel, putting his head on the Knight's shoulder.

"You're a sentimental dunce, Camy. I doubt whether they'll take us at all!" The Doubtful Dromedary looked wistfully at Dorothy.

"Go to, now!" cried Sir Hokus, putting an arm around each neck. "You're just like two of the family!"

"It will be very comfortable to go to now," sighed the camel.

"We're all a big, jolly family here," said the Scarecrow, smiling brightly, "and Oz is the friendliest country in the world."

"Right," said the Cowardly Lion, "but let's get started!" He stretched his tired muscles and began limping stiffly toward the yellow brick road.

"Wait," cried Dorothy, "have you forgotten the parasol?"

"I wish I could," groaned the Cowardly Lion, rolling his eyes.

Sir Hokus, with folded arms, was gazing regretfully at the bean pole. "It has been a brave quest," he sighed, "but now, I take it, our adventures are over!" Absently, the Knight felt in his boot-top and drawing out a small red bean popped it into his mouth. Just before reaching the top of the tube, he had pulled a handful of them from the beanstalk, but the others had fallen out when he dove into the hay.

"Shall we use the parasol again, Lady Dot?" he asked, still staring pensively at the bean pole. "Shall—?"

He got no farther, nor did Dorothy answer his question. Instead, she gave a loud scream and clutched the Scarecrow's arm. The Scarecrow, taken by surprise, fell over backward, and the Comfortable Camel, raising his head inquiringly, gave a bellow of terror. From the Knight's shoulders a green branch had sprung, and while the company gazed in round-eyed amazement it stretched toward the bean pole, attached itself firmly, and then shot straight up into the air, the Knight kicking and struggling on the end. In another second, he was out of sight.

"Come back! Come back!" screamed the Comfortable Camel, running around distractedly.

"I doubt we'll ever see him again!" groaned the Doubtful Dromedary, craning his neck upward.

"Do something! Do something!" begged Dorothy. At which the Scarecrow jumped up and dashed toward the little farmhouse.

"I'll get an axe," he called over his shoulder, "and chop down the bean pole."

"No, don't do that!" roared the Cowardly Lion, starting after him. "Do you want to break him to pieces?"

"Oh! Oh! Can't you think of something else?" cried Dorothy. "And hurry, or he'll be up to the moon!"

The Scarecrow put both hands to his head and stared around wildly. Then, with a triumphant wave of his hat, declared himself ready to act.

"The parasol!" cried the late Emperor of Silver Island. "Quick, Dorothy, put up the parasol!"

Snatching the parasol, which lay at the foot of the bean pole, Dorothy snapped it open, and the Scarecrow just had time to make a flying leap and seize the handle before it soared upward, and in a trice they, too, had disappeared.

"Doubty! Doubty!" wailed the Comfortable Camel, crowding up to his humpbacked friend, "we're having a pack of trouble. My knees are all atremble!"

"Now don't you worry," advised the Cowardly Lion, sitting down resignedly. "I'm frightened myself, but that's because I'm so cowardly. Queer things happen in Oz, but they usually turn out all right. Why, Hokus is just growing up with the country, that's all, just growing up with the country."

"Doubt that," sniffed the Doubtful Dromedary faintly. "He was grown up in the beginning."

"But think of the Scarecrow's brains. You leave things to the Scarecrow." But it was no use. Both beasts began to roar dismally.

"I don't want a plant. I want my Karwan Bashi," sobbed the Comfortable Camel broken-heartedly.

"Well, don't drown me," begged the Cowardly Lion, moving out of the way of the camel's tears. "Say, what's that draft?"

What indeed? In the trees overhead, a very cyclone whistled, and before the three had even time to catch their breath, they were blown high into the air and the next instant were hurtling toward the Emerald City like three furry cannonballs, faster and faster.

Chapter 24

Homeward Bound to the Emerald City

Dorothy and the Scarecrow, clinging fast to the magic parasol, had followed the Knight almost to the clouds. At first, it looked as if they would never catch up with him, so swiftly was the branch growing, but it was not long before the little umbrella began to gain, and in several minutes more they were beside Sir Hokus himself.

"Beshrew me, now!" gasped the Knight, stretching out his hand toward Dorothy. "Can'st stop this reckless plant?"

"Give me your sword," commanded the Scarecrow, "and I'll cut you off."

Dorothy, with great difficulty, kept the parasol close to the Knight while the Scarecrow reached for the sword. But Sir Hokus backed away in alarm.

"'Tis part of me, an' you cut it off, I will be cut

off, too. 'Tis rooted in my back," he puffed.

"What shall we do?" cried Dorothy in distress. "Maybe if we take hold of his hands we can keep him from going any higher."

The Scarecrow, jamming down his hat so it wouldn't blow off, nodded approvingly, and each holding the parasol with one hand gave the other to the Knight. And when Dorothy pointed the parasol down, to her great delight Sir Hokus came also, the thin green branch growing just about as fast as they moved.

Just then the little fan, which had been rolling around merrily in Dorothy's pocket, slipped out and fell straight down toward the three unsuspecting beasts below. Draft! No wonder!

But Dorothy never missed it, and quite unconscious of such a calamity anxiously talked over the Knight's predicament with the Scarecrow. They both decided that the best plan was to fly straight to the Emerald City and have Ozma release the Knight from the enchanted beanstalk.

"I'm sorry you got tangled up in my family tree, old fellow," said the Scarecrow after they had flown some time in silence, "but this makes us relations, doesn't it?" He winked broadly at the

Knight.

"So it does," said Sir Hokus jovially. "I'm a branch of your family now. Yet methinks I should not have swallowed that bean."

"Bean?" questioned Dorothy. "What bean?" The Knight carefully explained how he had plucked a handful of red beans from the beanstalk just before reaching the top of the tube and how he had eaten one.

"So that's what started you growing!" exclaimed Dorothy in surprise.

"Alas, yes!" admitted the Knight. "I've never felt more grown-up in my life," he finished solemnly. "An adventurous country, this Oz!"

"I should say it was," chuckled the Scarecrow. "But isn't it almost time we were reaching the Emerald City, Dorothy?"

"I think I'm going in the right direction," answered the little girl, "but I'll fly a little lower to be sure."

"Not too fast! Not too fast!" warned Sir Hokus, looking nervously over his shoulder at his long, wriggling stem.

"There's Ozma's palace!" cried the Scarecrow all at once.

"And there's Ozma!" screamed Dorothy, peering down delightedly. "And Scraps and Tik-Tok and everybody!"

She pointed the parasol straight down, when a sharp tug from Sir Hokus jerked them all back. They were going faster than the poor Knight was growing, so Dorothy lowered the parasol half way, and slowly they floated toward the earth, landing gently in one of the flower beds of Ozma's lovely garden.

"Come along and meet the folks," said the Scarecrow as Dorothy closed the parasol. But Sir Hokus clutched him in alarm.

"Hold! Hold!" gasped the Knight. "I've stopped growing, but if you leave me I'll shoot up into the air again."

The Scarecrow and Dorothy looked at each other in dismay. Sure enough, the Knight had stopped growing, and it was all they could do to hold him down to earth, for the stubborn branch of beanstalk was trying to straighten up. They had fallen quite a distance from the palace itself, and all the people of Oz had their backs turned, so had not seen their singular arrival.

"Hello!" called the Scarecrow loudly. Then "Help! Help!" as the Knight jerked him twice into the air. But Ozma, Trot, Jack Pumpkinhead and all the rest were staring upward and talking so busily among themselves that they did not hear either Dorothy's or the Scarecrow's cries. First one, then the other was snatched off his feet, and although Sir Hokus, with tears in his eyes, begged them to leave him to his fate, they held on with all their might. Just as it looked as if they all three would fly into the air again, the little Wizard of Oz happened to turn around.

"Look! Look!" he cried, tugging Ozma's sleeve.

"Why, it's Dorothy!" gasped Ozma, rubbing her eyes. "It's Dorothy and—"

"Help! Help!" screamed the Scarecrow, waving one arm wildly. Without waiting another second, all the celebrities of Oz came running toward the three adventurers.

"Somebody heavy come take hold!" puffed Dorothy, out of breath with her efforts to keep Sir Hokus on the ground.

The Ozites, seeing that help was needed at once, suppressed their curiosity.

"I'm heavy," said Tik-Tok solemnly, clasping the Knight's arm. The Tin Woodman seized his other hand, and Dorothy sank down exhausted on the grass.

Princess Ozma pressed forward. "What does it all mean? Where did you come from?" asked the little Queen of Oz, staring in amazement at the strange spectacle before her.

"And who is this medieval person?" asked Professor Wogglebug, pushing forward importantly. (He had returned to the palace to collect more data for the Royal Book of Oz.)

"He doesn't look evil to me," giggled Scraps, dancing up to Sir Hokus, her suspender button eyes snapping with fun.

"He isn't," said Dorothy indignantly, for Sir Hokus was too shaken about to answer. "He's my Knight Errant."

"Ah, I see," replied Professor Wogglebug. "A case of 'When Knighthood was in flower.'" And would you believe it—the beanstalk at that minute burst into a perfect shower of red blossoms that came tumbling down over everyone. Before they had recovered from their surprise, the branch snapped off close to the Knight's armour, and Tik-Tok, the Tin Woodman and Sir Hokus rolled over in a heap. The branch itself whistled through the air and disappeared.

"Oh," cried Dorothy, hugging the Knight impulsively, "I'm so glad."

"Are you all right?" asked the Scarecrow anxiously.

"Good as ever!" announced Sir Hokus, and indeed all traces of the magic stalk had disappeared from his shoulders.

"Dorothy!" cried Ozma again. "What does it all mean?"

"Merely that I slid down my family tree and that Dorothy and this Knight rescued me," said the Scarecrow calmly.

"And he's a real Royalty—so there!" cried Dorothy with a wave at the Scarecrow and making a little face at Professor Wogglebug. "Meet his Supreme Highness, Chang Wang Woe of Silver Island, who had abdicated his throne and returned to be a plain Scarecrow in Oz!"

Then, as the eminent Educator of Oz stood gaping at the Scarecrow, "Oh, Ozma, I've so much to tell you!"

"Begin! Begin!" cried the little Wizard. "For everything's mighty mysterious. First, the Cowardly Lion and two unknown beasts shoot through the air and stop just outside the third-story windows, and there they hang although I've tried all my magic to get them down. Then you and the Scarecrow drop in with a strange Knight!"

"Oh, the poor Cowardly Lion!" gasped Dorothy as the Wizard finished speaking. "The magic fan!" She felt hurriedly in her pocket. "It's gone!" "It must have slipped out of your pocket and blown them here, and they'll never come down till that fan is closed," cried the Scarecrow in an agitated voice.

All of this was Greek to Ozma and the others, but when Dorothy begged the little Queen to send for her Magic Belt, she did it without question. This belt Dorothy had captured from the Gnome King, and it enabled the wearer to wish people and objects wherever one wanted them.

"I wish the magic fan to close and to come safely back to me," said Dorothy as soon as she had clasped the belt around her waist. No sooner were the words out before there was a loud crash and a series of roars and groans. Everybody started on a run for the palace, Sir Hokus ahead of all the rest. The fan had mysteriously returned to Dorothy's pocket.

The three animals had fallen into a huge cluster of rose bushes and, though badly scratched and frightened, were really unhurt.

"I doubt that I'll like Oz," quavered the Doubtful Dromedary, lurching toward Sir Hokus.

"You might have been more careful of that fan," growled the Cowardly Lion reproachfully, plucking thorns from his hide. The Comfortable Camel was so overjoyed to see the Knight that he rested his head on Sir Hokus's shoulder and began weeping down his armour.

And now that their adventures seemed really over, what explanations were to be made! Sitting on the top step of the palace with all of them around her, Dorothy told the whole wonderful story of the Scarecrow's family tree. When her breath gave out, the Scarecrow took up the tale himself, and as they all realized how nearly they had lost their jolly comrade, many of the party shed real tears. Indeed, Nick Chopper hugged the Scarecrow till there was not a whole straw in his body.

"Never leave us again," begged Ozma, and the Scarecrow, crossing Nick Chopper's heart (he had none of his own), promised that he never would.

And what a welcome they gave Sir Hokus, the Doubtful Dromedary and the Comfortable Camel! Only Professor Wogglebug seemed disturbed.

During the strange recital, he had grown quieter and quieter and finally, with an embarrassed cough, had excused himself and hurried into the palace.

He went directly to the study, and seating himself at a desk opened a large book, none other than The Royal Book of Oz. Dipping an emerald pen in the ink, he began a new chapter headed thus:

HIS IMPERIAL MAJESTY, THE SCARECROW
Late Emperor and Imperial Sovereign of Silver Islands

Then, flipping over several pages to a chapter headed "Princess Dorothy!", he wrote carefully at the end, "Dorothy, Princess and Royal Discoverer of Oz."

Meanwhile, below stairs, the Scarecrow was distributing his gifts. There were silver chains for everyone in the palace and shining silver slippers for Ozma, Betsy Bobbin, Trot and Dorothy, and a bottle of silver polish for Nick Chopper.

Dorothy presented Ozma with the magic fan and parasol, and they were safely put away by Jellia Jamb with the other magic treasures of Oz. Next, because they were all curious to see the Scarecrow's wonderful Kingdom, they hurried upstairs to look in the Magic Picture.

"Show us the Emperor of Silver Island," commanded Ozma. Immediately the beautiful silver throne room appeared. Happy Toko had removed his imperial hat and was standing on his head to the great delight of the whole court, and a host of little Silver Islander boys were peeking in at the windows.

"Now doesn't that look cheerful?" asked the Scarecrow delightedly. "I knew he'd make a good Emperor."

"I wish we would hear what he's saying," said Dorothy. "Oh, do look at Chew Chew!" The Grand Chew Chew was standing beside the throne scowling horribly.

"I think I can arrange for you to hear," muttered the Wizard of Oz, and taking a queer magic instrument from his pocket, he whispered "Aohbeeobbuy."

Instantly they heard the jolly voice of Happy Toko singing:

> *"Oh shine his shoes of silver,*
> *And brush his silver queue,*
> *For I am but an Emperor*
> *And he's the Grand Chew Chew!"*

Ozma laughed heartily as the picture faded away, and so did the others. Indeed, there was so much to ask and wonder about that it seemed as if they never would finish talking.

"Let's have a party—an old-fashioned Oz party," proposed Ozma when the excitement had calmed down a bit. And an old-fashioned party it was, with places for everybody and a special table for the Cowardly Lion, the Hungry Tiger, Toto, the Glass Cat, the Comfortable Camel, the Doubtful Dromedary and all the other dear creatures of that amazing Kingdom.

Sir Hokus insisted upon stirring up a huge pasty for the occasion, and there were songs, speeches and cheers for everyone, not forgetting the Doubtful Dromedary.

At the cheering he rose with an embarrassed jerk of his long neck. "In my left-hand saddle-sack," he said gruffly, "there is a quantity of silken shawls and jewels. I doubt whether they are good enough, but I would like Dorothy and Queen Ozma to have them."

"Hear! Hear!" cried the Scarecrow, pounding on the table with his knife. Then everything grew quiet as Ozma told how she, with the help of Glinda, the Good Sorceress, had stopped the war between the Horners and Hoppers.

When she had finished, Sir Hokus sprang up impulsively. "I prithee, lovely Lady, never trouble your royal head about wars again. From now on, I will do battle for you and little Dorothy and Oz, and I will be your good Knight every day." At this, the applause was tremendous.

"Ye good Knight of Oz, full of courage and vim,
Will do battle for us, and we'll take care of him!"

shouted Scraps, who was becoming more excited every minute.

"I'll lend you some of my polish for your armour, old fellow," said Nick Chopper as the Knight sat down, beaming with pleasure.

"Well," said Ozma with a smile when everyone had feasted and talked to heart's content, "is everybody happy?"

"I am!" cried the Comfortable Camel. "For here I am perfectly comfortable."

"I am!" cried Dorothy, putting her arm around the Scarecrow, who sat next to her. "For I have found my old friend and made some new ones."

"I'm happy!" cried the Scarecrow, waving his glass, "because there is no age in Oz, and I am still my old Ozish self."

"As for me," said the Knight, "I am happy, for I have served a Lady, gone on a Quest, and Slain a Dragon! Ozma, and Oz forever!"

Also Available:

The Wonderful Wizard of Oz
978-1-78226-061-5

The Marvellous Land of Oz
978-1-78226-062-2

Ozma of Oz
978-1-78226-063-9

Dorothy and the Wizard in Oz
978-1-78226-064-6

The Road to Oz
978-1-78226-097-4

The Emerald City of Oz
978-1-78226-098-1

The Patchwork Girl of Oz
978-1-78226-099-8

The Wizard of Oz Collection

THE WONDERFUL WIZARD OF OZ

Book One

The Wonderful Wizard of Oz